JENNIFER S. ALDERSON

Death by Windmill

A Mother's Day Murder in Amsterdam

First published by Traveling Life Press 2020

Copyright © 2020 by Jennifer S. Alderson

This novel is entirely a work of fiction. The names, characters and incidents portrayed in it are the work of the author's imagination. Any resemblance to actual persons, living or dead, events or localities is entirely coincidental.

First edition

ISBN: 9798646330070

This book was professionally typeset on Reedsy.
Find out more at reedsy.com

To my mother, Cherie, one of my favorite traveling companions.

Contents

1

Mothers and Daughters

March 20—Seattle, Washington

"Are you one hundred percent positive that Gillian won't mind you working on Mother's Day?" Dotty Thompson asked. From her tone, it was evident that she did not believe a word Lana Hansen was saying.

Dotty was finalizing her roster of guides for several upcoming tours and was now wishy-washy about allowing Lana to lead the Mother's Day tour of the Netherlands. Since recently discovering that Lana and her mother were estranged, Dotty had made it her mission to bring them back together and seemed to think the upcoming holiday was the perfect time to do so. As much as Lana loved Dotty, she was having a tough time figuring out how to tell the older lady to butt out.

"I am quite certain. We haven't celebrated the day together in several years. Ten, to be exact," Lana replied. Even though they lived only a few miles apart, her mother could have lived in Alaska for all it mattered. They never made time for each other, and Lana was the first to admit that both were to blame.

Dotty leaned against her apple tree, recovering from the shock. Dotty's pug and Jack Russell terrier chose that moment to play tug-of-war with one of the colorful paper streamers strewn across the lawn. As they growled and shook their jaws, bits of the decorations flew off, sending a shower of rainbow-colored confetti across the lawn.

Lana groaned in irritation. Their playfulness was only making it more difficult to clean up after last night's spring equinox party. Dotty's backyard had been filled with neighbors happy to ring in the return of spring with a glass of bubbly and finger foods, while their children ran and played among Dotty's fruit trees.

"Okay, boys, that's enough." Lana tried to wrestle the colorful streamer out of the dogs' mouths, but they misinterpreted her attempt to clean up as playtime. They growled and yelped as she slowly loosened the decorations from their muzzles. After Lana had taken away their toy, the two dogs moved on to tag, yapping in delight as they chased each other around the yard.

Lana's cat, Seymour, rubbed against her leg, purring as he watched the dogs play. When Seymour sniffed a tiny scrap of paper and tentatively tasted it, Lana shooed him away and redoubled her cleaning efforts.

"Besides, I have always wanted to visit the Netherlands, and you already have me scheduled to lead it. Please don't ground me. It won't force me to look Gillian up. We haven't spoken in so long, she wouldn't be expecting me to get in touch, even on Mother's Day," Lana pleaded.

"I cannot believe you haven't celebrated Mother's Day with Gillian in over a decade." Dotty shook her head slowly, seemingly stuck on Lana's initial answer. "She is your *mother*, after all. And you both live in Seattle, for goodness' sake."

Lana shrugged. "We were never close. After I got fired from the newspaper, our contact dissipated pretty quickly. I think she is ashamed to admit that I am her daughter." One look at Dotty's distraught expression made her add, "I can't blame her; Gillian's world is advertising and perception. After the *Seattle Chronicle* lost the libel suit and fired me, I was in the news a lot, but never in a positive light."

Lana closed her eyes, recalling those dark days. Soon after she had been sacked, her mother had stopped taking Lana's calls. Gillian was her only relative on the West Coast, which made her rejection even more painful. Her father's family was spread across the East Coast and she had lost touch with most of them since her dad's death twenty years ago.

Dotty pulled Lana in for a hug. "Her job doesn't give her an excuse to leave you high and dry. How could she not love you? You are so smart, creative, and rational. If you were my flesh and blood, I would tell everyone I met how wonderful you are."

"Sometimes I wish you were my biological mother, Dotty," Lana confessed, relaxing into the older lady's embrace. They had only lived under the same roof for a year, but most days, Dotty felt more like her mother than Gillian ever had.

"It's just not right." Dotty shook her head sadly.

"Giving birth to a child is not a guarantee that you will become best friends, Dotty," Lana gently reminded her.

Lana knew not being able to have children was a cross Dotty bore. She was a wonderful stepmother to six grown sons, but on Mother's Day, the kids always treated their biological mothers to breakfast, not Dotty. For Dotty, it was one of the most painful days of the year. Lana's only regret in leading this tour was that she wouldn't be in Seattle on Mother's Day to help brighten up her friend's day.

"If you are sure Gillian won't mind, then you are welcome to be the lead guide on the Holland tour. Since only women have booked spaces, I did ask Randy to be the second guide. I figure you could use a little testosterone on the trip," Dotty cackled.

Lana sighed in relief. "Thanks, Dotty."

She was really looking forward to seeing the Netherlands and, in particular, Amsterdam. The historic windmills, many canals, grand homes, and plethora of bicycles seemed so romantic and charming. It would also be fun to work with Randy again. He was one of the most laid-back guides employed by Wanderlust Tours at the moment. After bonding during a tour in France, they had gotten together regularly when both were back in Seattle. Lana also got along well with his girlfriend, Gloria, a spunky Italian beauty who was a beehive of activity and positivity that was perfect for him. Lana wouldn't be surprised if they tied the knot later this year.

Most of all, Lana was glad this trip gave her a good excuse not to get together with Gillian. After not speaking for almost two years, her mother had recently begun following Lana's social media accounts. In Gillian's world, this was a way of saying hello. So far, Lana had ignored her and not followed her back or acknowledged her likes. Lana hadn't told Dotty about this recent surge of activity for fear that she would ground her until she and Gillian met face to face. *If Gillian really wanted to talk to me, she could pick up the phone*, Lana thought, as she tied off one garbage bag and grabbed another.

2

Surprise at the Check-In Counter

May 2—Seattle, Washington

Lana and Randy strolled into SeaTac Airport, relaxed in the knowledge that they were a half hour early for their check-in to Amsterdam. It had been good to catch up with her fellow tour guide on the monorail ride over. He had recently returned from two weeks in southern Spain and was nicely tanned from his hikes through the Pyrenees and walks through Granada, Cordoba, and Seville. It sounded like a wonderful area of the world. Lana hoped that the next time Dotty offered the Andalusia tour, she would consider Lana for one of the guide positions.

Randy was always enthusiastic, but on the ride over, he couldn't stop grinning from ear to ear. When Lana pressed him for more information, all he would say was that a special visitor was joining them.

Whatever Randy had planned, Lana hoped it did not involve a romantic setup. Since her mishap with a singles dating website three months earlier, Lana had given up on finding romance online. Instead, she had given her friends free rein to set her up. She couldn't have foreseen the plethora of potential suitors they lined up for her. Whenever she was back in Seattle, they conspired to set her up with a different blind date for every night of the week.

Randy had also contributed a name to the list—a nice guy who didn't interest Lana in the slightest. The most embarrassing part of having her friends recommend dates was having to later explain to Randy, Willow, Jane, Dotty, and the rest why their choices were not perfect. It was often more challenging than she expected. To add to her frustration, in a few cases, Dotty had actually invited the men to come over for tea the next day, so Lana could have a second shot at making it work.

As much as she appreciated her friends' help, she was not the type of person to fall in love for the sake of being with someone. If her divorce had taught her anything, it was that finding the right partner was far more important than grabbing onto the first eligible single who entered her crosshairs.

After they found the right check-in gate inside of the chaotic and bustling airport, Randy began speed walking as if he was trying to beat Lana to the desk. Figuring it was his way of being silly, Lana matched his pace and speed, grinning back at him as she passed him. Randy chuckled while looking ahead, then suddenly froze in place as that goofy grin of his returned. Lana slowed her stride and followed his gaze.

A few feet away were Dotty and her friend Sally. Lana's jaw dropped in shock. When Lana had asked Dotty about her Mother's Day plans, she'd been unusually vague. Never in a million years had Lana thought she was going to join the Netherlands trip.

Dotty had not been abroad in more than a year, ever since a nasty cold had kept her in her hotel room instead of leading a tour group through Prague. The other guide had been more than capable of taking care of their clients. Yet, as the owner of Wanderlust Tours, Dotty had been so mortified by her own infirmity and inability to push on that she'd hung up her guide hat as soon as she got back to Seattle. The last thing she wanted was to be a burden to anyone. Since then, she had focused her efforts on marketing and creating unique, thematic tours.

"What the heck? Are you two joining us in Holland?" Lana pulled her landlord in for a hug. "I hope you'll be happy with how Randy and I lead the tour."

"Don't worry—I'm not here to check up on you two," Dotty said. "Sally and I have been talking about going traveling again for quite some time, and

I figured this was a great way to ease back into it. I know the tour is fuller than normal, but you won't have to worry about me and Sally. We can take care of ourselves."

"What about our boys?" Lana said, remembering that Dotty was supposed to be caring for their pets while Lana was in the Netherlands.

"Rodney, Chipper, and Seymour are in great hands. Willow is going to stay at my place and take care of them for us. Wasn't that sweet of her to offer?"

Lana nodded, relaxed in the knowledge that her cat would be well taken care of. Willow was Lana's best friend and the perfect person to care for Dotty's dogs and Lana's cat while they were away.

"That sure was nice of Willow. Oh, it's going to be great to have you on the tour. And Sally's here!" Lana hugged her as well. "It's so good to see you. Since you took up with your new boyfriend, I haven't seen you at Dotty's place as much."

Sally and Dotty were best friends as well as business partners. Together they knitted a successful line of clothes for canines called Doggone Gorgeous. Sally had also been a guest on Lana's first trip as a guide, and they had bonded during their week in Budapest. Lana was glad to hear that Sally had gotten over her cheating boyfriend Carl and had settled down with a kind, older man who shared all of her interests—except travel.

"Yeah, well, he is pretty wonderful." Sally blushed. "It's only too bad he doesn't like to fly. That's why Dotty asked me to join her on this trip. Isn't that sweet?"

"I did bring a bunch of wool and was hoping we could talk through a few new design ideas I have, as well," Dotty added, patting her gigantic handbag. "Since you and your new beau moved in together, we haven't been knitting as much."

"I hope you don't having any knitting needles in there," Lana said, recalling how sharp Sally's travel needles were from their trip to Budapest. "Security won't let you take them on the plane."

"Oh, you have a point there. I better put them into my suitcase before we check in." Dotty opened the bag closest to her, a large red suitcase that was almost as tall as she was. *Thank goodness it had wheels*, Lana thought, *otherwise Dotty wouldn't be able to move it around on her own.* Lana knew from experience how handy luggage with wheels was. She had recently traded in her vintage suitcase for a smaller bag with wheels and a combo lock, and she had been pleasantly surprised by how much nicer it was to roll her case instead of having to lug it around.

Lana took in the second large suitcase and pair of backpacks next to Dotty. "Wow, you have a lot of luggage with you," she said, concerned about how they were going to get all of it to the hotel. She and Randy would have to help. Luckily, Sally had brought only one along.

Dotty chuckled. "Those two aren't mine. I have another surprise for you," she said while glancing towards the bathroom door close to the check-in desk.

Lana's brow furrowed, and Dotty smiled slyly in response. "You're just going to have to wait a few more minutes for it to appear."

Was another guide joining them because the tour group was so large? Dotty did tend to prefer a maximum ratio of five guests to one guide. And they had eleven confirmed guests already on the tour, excluding Sally and Dotty. Though why that should be a surprise was beyond Lana.

Lana looked to the bathroom, wondering what else Dotty had in store for her, when the door opened, and a tall, smartly dressed woman in her mid-sixties walked out.

"Oh, no." Lana cringed at the sight as a wave of anger rose up inside her. Why did Dotty have to try to fix everything she deemed broken? Why couldn't she leave well enough alone?

"Surprise!" Dotty yelled as the woman walked towards them.

"Hi, Mom. Long time, no see." Lana tried her best to keep her tone neutral.

Gillian Hansen looked down on her daughter, her lips pursed as she took in Lana's comfortable clothes, ponytail, and lack of makeup. "Lana. It's good to see you."

She held out her hand just as Lana reached out to hug her. Both stepped back awkwardly, unsure how to proceed.

"Are you, um, coming to Amsterdam with us?" Lana asked, reddening as her voice cracked. They hadn't spoken in almost two years, and that last conversation had been anything but civil. She had no idea what her mother was doing here and wondered what Dotty must have said to get her to agree to come.

Gillian nodded stiffly and looked away.

"Great," Lana said, though her tone was anything but enthusiastic. She had been so looking forward to this trip, but the thought of Gillian on it was causing her excitement to dissipate rapidly.

Dotty stepped in between them and laid her arms over Gillian and Lana's shoulders. "Your mom wants to join us. Isn't this special? Now you will get to spend Mother's Day together," she said, giving them both a million-watt smile before releasing them from her embrace.

"Sure. Hey, Dotty, can I talk to you for a minute?" Lana said and took ten steps away from her biological mother, not caring what Gillian thought.

Dotty followed, yet from her puzzled expression, she truly didn't understand Lana's lukewarm reaction to her mother's presence.

"Is she really coming on the trip I'm leading? We are already overbooked, and Gillian is high maintenance. I can't focus my attention on her; you pay me to look out for all my guests, not just one."

"Which is the real reason why Sally and I are joining you. I don't trust myself to lead a tour anymore, but I am more than capable of helping out with the day trips. And this time around, I figure you and Randy can split up the group into two small ones, so that each of you has less to worry about. I have also asked Randy to be the lead guide on this tour, so you have more time for Gillian."

"You what?" Lana closed her eyes and took a deep, cleansing breath. Lana knew Randy was more than capable of taking the lead, but she was a bit put out that Dotty had made her second fiddle without even asking her first.

"It's important that you make time for your mom. You only get one," Dotty said while smiling nervously, as if she was finally aware that she may have gone too far.

"I don't know, Dotty. I can't really get to know Gillian again while I'm working. Your clients pay quite a bit of money to be pampered. You can't expect me to ignore them to spend time with her." Lana could hear how her own voice rose in pitch as her desperation intensified, but she couldn't help it. Spending ten days with her estranged mother was the last thing she wanted to do.

Dotty put her hands on her hips. "Lana Hansen, what is wrong with you? Your mom and I talked a few times, and she seems nice enough. Most importantly, she wants to be here."

"Wait—did you ask her to join us, or did she call you?"

"I called her, but she was quite receptive to the idea. It just took her a little time to confirm that she could join us for the full ten days, that's all."

"Odd. I figured you blackmailed her into coming somehow."

Dotty looked up at Lana in shock and sadness. "I know you are a bit wary because you haven't spoken much since you got fired. But this is your chance to reconnect with her. Don't shut her out, Lana. You'll always regret it if you do. And what a better time to get to know each other again than during a Mother's Day trip? Amsterdam is one of our easiest tours, which makes it an ideal one to have Gillian join us on."

Knowing she had no choice in the matter, Lana nodded curtly, then glanced at her mother, watching them like a hawk, a frown settled firmly on her face. It was going to be a long ten days.

3

Barbs and Accusations

May 2—Day One of the Wanderlust Tour in Amsterdam, the Netherlands

The plane ride over was tense, to say the least. Randy insisted on switching seats with Gillian—despite both her and Lana's protests—meaning they had to pretend to get along for eleven hours. Considering they hadn't spoken amicably to each other in quite some time, it was a challenge. They had so much to discuss and catch up on, yet neither knew where to start. Every topic was met with suspicion by the other, on the lookout for hidden barbs and unspoken accusations.

Dotty and Sally sat behind them, and anytime there was a lull in the conversation, Dotty sprung in and started asking all sorts of questions to get the ball rolling again. Nothing really worked. After a few hours of trying, even Dotty gave up and settled into a nap. Lana and Gillian read for the rest of the flight, using their paperbacks as shields for the remainder of the trip.

Schiphol Airport was massive but incredibly easy to get around. The Dutch really had an eye for design and organization. *If this airport was any indication of how the rest of the country operates, this is going to be an incredibly relaxed trip,* Lana thought.

They breezed through customs and followed the crowds to baggage claim. As they waited for their luggage to arrive, Lana, Randy, and Dotty turned on their phones. All three began beeping.

Dotty was the first to find out why. "Well, that's too bad. Two of our guests won't be able to join us. It's one of the ladies from your Budapest trip and her daughter."

"Oh, no, it's not Frieda, is it?" Lana had been excited to see Frieda, Sara, and Rebecca again—three of the five ladies who called themselves the "Fabulous Five." Frieda was probably the most abrasive of the bunch, but for some reason, Lana had warmed to her the most.

"No, Rebecca. She has a nasty cough and is worried it might be bronchitis or pneumonia."

"That's too bad, but I understand. It would be terrible to get truly ill while traveling, and Rebecca is in her seventies."

"Lana, I need to make a call. I'll be right back," Gillian announced as she set her luggage down next to her daughter and took several steps away before dialing.

"Okay," Lana acknowledged, then turned her attention back to Dotty.

"Them not being here might be a blessing in disguise," her boss reasoned. "It will make the group more manageable, in any case. Though I'm still not opposed to splitting the group into two, if it makes it easier for you and Randy."

"Great, he can entertain Gillian."

"Lana," Dotty admonished, "you can't reconnect with your mother if you avoid her. Let her get to know you as a person again. When I talked with her on the phone, I was downright shocked by how little she knows about your life. She didn't even know you were working for me as a guide. Did she ever meet Ron?"

"Yeah, she did, though she didn't approve of him. I suppose that was another strike against me—marrying a magician shortly after getting fired. According to Gillian, he was far beneath me and I should have held out for better."

Dotty snorted. "The heart wants what the heart wants."

"I suppose. Trust me, at that time in my life, Ron was the perfect companion. If I hadn't met him when I did, I would probably still be wallowing in self-pity. We were so busy with the show and touring, I never had time to sit around and feel sorry for myself. And performing on stage was a lot more invigorating than I ever imagined."

"That must be why you are so good at leading these tours. You're a natural performer."

Lana stopped to consider her remark. She had never thought about leading the groups as being similar to her work as a magician's assistant, but Dotty was right. It was essentially being on stage for most of the day, pretending to be a friendlier version of her true self. "Maybe it is," she conceded.

Moments later, Gillian finished her call, and the motley crew headed out to find a taxi to their hotel.

4

Switching Rooms

Lana and Randy stood in the hotel's grand lobby, waiting for the rest of their guests to arrive. Dotty and Sally were seated in wingback chairs with knitting projects out on their laps. Gillian sat next to them, but her attention was focused on the window overlooking a street and canal, bustling with boats, pedestrians, cars, trams, and bicycles.

Her mother had changed out of her emerald pantsuit and into another one of the characteristically bright outfits she favored. This afternoon's ensemble was a tailored jacket and shirt made from fire-engine red fabric. *At least I won't have trouble spotting her in the crowds*, Lana thought.

Lana looked out the window and took in the glorious morning. Their hotel was situated along the Herengracht, one of the larger canals circling the city's horseshoe-shaped center. As she noticed the trees lining the waterway, Lana was again surprised to see how green the city was. There were trees and flowers everywhere. Considering almost a million people lived within Amsterdam's compact city center, Lana had figured greenery would be limited to a few city parks.

The first guests to arrive were Frieda and Sara. Trailing slowly behind them was a younger, rather drab woman. A smile sprung to Lana's face as soon as the two older ladies entered the lobby. They had helped make her first trip as a guide a fun experience, and she was incredibly glad to see them again. Dotty had mentioned to Lana on the plane that Frieda's daughter

14

would be joining them on the second day of the tour. Lana made a mental note to ask Frieda about it later as she rushed over to them, excited to see her former clients again.

Frieda wrapped her up in a bear hug, rocking her back and forth like a long-lost child. "It is so good to see you, young lady!"

"It is great to see you and Sara, as well!" Lana said as she wormed her way out of Frieda's embrace and into Sara's arms.

When Sara released Lana, she turned to the younger woman standing next to them and said with pride, "This is my daughter, Anne."

Lana held out her hand. "Hi, I'm Lana, one of the guides on this tour. It's nice to meet you."

Anne barely made eye contact as she shook Lana's hand. When she released Lana's grip, Anne pushed a strand of stringy hair over her ear. She was wearing a loose-fitting peasant dress over sweatpants that probably hadn't been washed in weeks. Considering how upbeat and stylish Sara was, Lana was quite surprised to learn that this girl was her daughter.

"Lana took such great care of us in Budapest, didn't she, Sara?" Frieda enthused. "Being a guide must suit you, Lana. You look younger somehow." Frieda held her at arm's length, studying Lana's face and hair.

"Why, thank you," Lana responded, thinking, of course I do, I didn't have to color my hair gray this time.

When Dotty had asked her to fill in as guide on the Budapest tour last December, it came with the stipulation that Lana had to dye her hair gray in order to appease the guests' specific request for an older guide. She was grateful that she didn't have to repeat that procedure this time around.

"I just found out that Rebecca and her daughter won't be joining us. That's such a shame that Rebecca got sick, but I understand her hesitance to travel right now. I hope she feels better soon. Will you let her know that I'm thinking about her, when you talk to her next?" Lana looked to Frieda and Sara for confirmation.

Frieda snorted. "Is that what she told you—that she's ill?" Her voice rose as more guests entered the lobby. "No, she and her daughter got into a blowup over her daughter's deadbeat boyfriend. Rebecca knows he is the wrong person for her but can't get her daughter to understand why. Heck, she wanted her daughter to come on this trip, in the hopes that if she got her away from the guy, she could talk some sense into her."

"When Rebecca told her she'd booked this trip and expected her to come along, her daughter called her all sorts of horrible names, then took off. Last we heard, she still hasn't gotten in touch with Rebecca," Sara added.

"I'm afraid if she keeps going out with him, Rebecca might disinherit her, in an attempt to get her attention," Frieda finished.

Lana was about to respond when she noticed one of the newly arrived guests was listening to their conversation, her mouth agape. *That's odd*, she thought, before the younger blonde woman noticed Lana watching and walked away.

Lana started to turn back to Sara when she spotted Randy working his way around the room, introducing himself to the new arrivals. Lana was glad to be working with him again; Randy was one of the friendliest guides she had met and was always willing to jump in and help out, without having to be asked.

"I better say hi to everyone before our taxi gets here. Hopefully on the boat we'll have a chance to talk more."

"No problem, Lana. We are just tickled pink to spend a week with you again," Sara said, beaming in delight.

Lana squeezed her hand. "Me, too, Sara. Though I do hope this trip is not as deadly as Budapest was."

"Us, too," Frieda laughed.

When Sally and Dotty entered the lobby, Frieda waved them over. "Speak of the devil! Why, Sally, it is so good to see you."

Sara, Sally, and Frieda had all been guests on Lana's Budapest trip, during which they'd gotten along like a house on fire. As she walked away, she heard Sara ask, "So, Sally, how are you holding up since Carl died?"

To say his murder had put a damper on their trip to Budapest was the understatement of the year. Lana was just glad that Sally had ultimately been cleared of the crime. She was turning back to listen to Sally's answer, when a woman's voice rising in irritation attracted her attention.

"I don't want to hear your excuses. The view from our room is substandard, and I want to know what you are going to do about it. We expected better from Wanderlust Tours. We are paying quite a bit to be here, you know."

Lana was shocked to hear a guest complaining already, and about the hotel room, to boot. The Mansion was located in a beautifully restored historic building in the heart of the city, and the rooms were fitted with every modern convenience. What was there to complain about?

As her eyes scanned the lobby for the source of the complaint, she noticed Dotty bristling. *Poor Dotty*, she thought, *this is not the way she would want one of her tours to begin.*

Lana locked in on Randy, standing with two guests on the other side of the room. He seemed to be attempting to engage the complaining guest in a normal conversation, without much success. Apparently his mellow approach wasn't working with this client.

Knowing how important it was to cut off the complainers before their negativity affected the group, Lana rushed over to him. The complainer was standing with another woman. Based on their age difference, Lana assumed they were mother and daughter. The daughter was using her phone to snap pictures of the lobby while her mother stood with her arms crossed over her torso and a frown on her face.

Both were dressed in matching outfits that could only be described as thrift store chic. Unfortunately for the mother, the clothing's style and size was far more suited to the daughter. Both women had teased their long black hair into beehive buns that would have made Amy Winehouse proud.

Most notable were the plethora of bracelets and necklaces the mother and daughter wore. The expensive-looking glass beads seemed to be randomly strung together on thin metal wires and clashed horribly with their stylish outfits. They reminded Lana of something a kid would make during an arts and crafts class.

Lana held her hand out to the mother. "Hi, I am Lana Hansen. Are you booked in with Wanderlust Tours? Randy and I will be leading the tour of the Netherlands this week. How can we help you?"

Because Randy was technically the lead guide on this trip, Lana was slightly concerned he would be offended by her stepping in. Yet based on how he moved back to give her room, he apparently didn't mind.

The mother ignored her hand but did turn to face Lana, effectively blocking Randy out of her view. "Our rooms look out onto another building and not the canal. We spent thousands of dollars to come here, and I expect to see water from my window. If I wanted a brick wall, I would have booked a cheaper tour." Her voice rose even higher as she spoke. When she finished her rant, the entire lobby was staring at her.

Lana put on her most charismatic smile. "Of course, let me see what I can do for you. Which rooms are you in now?"

"I'm in room 3, and my daughter is in room 5. We both want views of the canal."

"Great. And your names are?"

"Wait, if you are leading this tour, why don't you know our names?" the mother asked, her voice filled with suspicion.

"I receive a list of names and passport numbers, but not photographs," Lana said as neutrally as possible. Over the past few months, she had learned that every tour had at least one difficult guest; apparently this woman would fill that role on this trip. Unfortunately, the daughter didn't seem to notice her mother's tantrum, keeping her attention focused on her phone rather than helping defuse the situation.

"Let me talk to the hotel's reception desk and get your rooms sorted, okay?" The woman in room 3 nodded slightly.

When Lana walked over to the reception desk, the hotel employee already had two new keys in her hand.

"I take it you heard all that? I'm not sure who those two women are, but they are staying in rooms 3 and 5."

"How could I not. That is Tammy and Hadley Peters. The mother specifically requested rooms on the lowest floor, in case of fire. I did tell her that she would not have a canal view, but she apparently didn't listen." The hotel employee smirked in Tammy's direction. "We do have two rooms available on the top floor, and both look out onto the Herengracht. If that doesn't make your guests happy, you will have to move them to a different hotel."

"No, that won't be necessary. I know this is one of the best hotels in Amsterdam. It's them, not you," Lana reassured the woman as she groaned internally. Apparently Tammy had already made her presence known. The last thing she wanted was the hotel employees to treat her guests badly based on the behavior of one bad egg.

"Please ask them to turn in their keys as soon as they've moved their belongings," the receptionist said as she pushed the two keys towards Lana. She leaned over the desk, adding softly, "Good luck with those two."

"Thanks, I think I'll need it," Lana whispered back.

She walked back to her guests, hoping this change would satisfy them. "Here are keys to rooms with a view of the canal. After we get back from the day's tours, you can move your things to the new rooms, alright?"

"I want to do that now," Tammy insisted.

"I'm sorry, but that's not possible, unless you want to skip the canal tour. Our taxis just arrived," Lana said, nodding towards the two minibus-style taxi cabs pulling up in front of the hotel. "I can't delay the boat."

"Humph. A real guide would have offered to move our things for us before we left. I do miss the days of maidservants." The woman stormed off towards the taxis with her daughter in tow.

All Lana could do was shake her head. *At least I've identified the troublemaker right away*, she thought.

5

Cruising the Canals of Amsterdam

As her group stepped into the sleek canal boat Dotty had reserved for their first adventure in Amsterdam, Lana couldn't help but smile. It was a beautiful spring day. Sunlight danced on the water, birds were singing, and the trees were full of budding green leaves.

As Lana waited to board, she took in the grand homes lining Amsterdam's famous canals. Several looked like extravagant dollhouses. They were so narrow and tall, with gorgeous scrollwork and wooden shutters around the windows. Sticking out of the tops were thick pieces of wood with a hook on the end, for winches and pulley systems. Most buildings were topped with extravagant gables. Some looked like staircases climbing over the tops of the homes, while others reminded Lana of bells.

Through the boat's many glass windows, she could see her guests splitting up to sit at the tables lining both sides of the vessel. Three guests made a beeline to the table at the back. Based on their ages, Lana assumed it was a mother and two daughters. The dark-haired daughter greatly resembled her mother, yet the blonde one did not. *She must take after her father*, Lana thought. When she looked more closely, she realized the blonde was the same woman who had reacted so strongly to her conversation with Frieda about Rebecca and her daughter arguing.

Lana felt bad that she didn't yet know all of her guests' names, but she had been too busy with Tammy to introduce herself to everyone. She hoped

Dotty or Randy knew who these three were.

Frieda, Sara, and Anne gravitated towards the middle of the boat. Tammy and Hadley took seats at the table across from them.

Gillian sat at a table close to the boat's entrance, and Dotty and Sally immediately joined her. Lana swore she saw a wave of irritation pass over her mother's face, and it filled her with shame. The last thing she needed was for Gillian to treat Dotty and Sally as if they were lesser. Lana felt closer to those two quirky yet wonderful women than she did to Gillian. Without Dotty's friendship, Lana doubted she would have recovered so quickly from her divorce.

Lana stepped into the boat and tapped Gillian's table with her knuckle. "Save me a place, will you?" She smiled at the three women; only Dotty and Sally smiled back.

"Are we eating on the boat, too?" Gillian asked. She sat stiffly on the edge of her chair and kept her hands in her lap.

To Lana, Gillian's body language made clear how uncomfortable and out of her element her mother felt. Though Gillian regularly crisscrossed the continental United States for her work, she rarely traveled abroad.

"No, this is just a short cruise introducing us to the city," Dotty responded. "The captain will drop us off at the Museum of Bags and Purses for its famous high tea."

"Bags and purses? That sounds more like a shop than a museum to me." Gillian laughed. "Couldn't you find any place fancier to have lunch?"

Lana bit hard on her tongue, and based on Dotty's expression, she was doing the same.

"The museum has one of the poshest high teas I've ever had, outside of England anyway. I bet you'll love it," Dotty said, patting Gillian's hand.

Lana's mother pulled her arm back so quickly it was as if she'd been burned.

Lana locked eyes with Dotty, attempting to convey "I told you so," with her expression. "Let me get everyone settled, then I'll be back," she said aloud, instead.

While she took her guests' drink orders, Randy handed them all a copy of their long itinerary. It was too bad that Rebecca and her daughter weren't able to join them for the trip, but it was nice to have a smaller group, Lana realized. Dotty claimed that the Netherlands tour was one of the easiest because the country was so small. The short distances between major cities meant they could visit several tourist hot spots in one day without wearing their guests out. Because of this, Dotty had packed more into this itinerary than most. Despite Dotty's reassurances that everything would work out fine, Lana hoped everyone would be able to keep up with the pace.

When Randy was finished passing out the itineraries, he approached Frieda, Sara, and Anne. "Is this seat taken?" he asked.

"Of course not! Heck, we're happy to have the man of the tour join us." Frieda patted the empty seat next to her and across from Anne. When he sat and smiled at his guests, Anne grinned back. Lana was amazed to see his friendly gesture actually got a positive response out of the otherwise sullen woman.

"So, Randy, is it? How long have you been a guide?" Frieda asked.

Lana laughed internally as she walked to the beverage bar at the back. Randy was in good hands with the older women, and he might even be able to get Anne to come out of her shell.

When she took drinks to Hadley and Tammy's table, she wondered whether Tammy would approve of this cruise. Based on her sour expression, it didn't appear to be the case. On the other hand, Hadley had her phone out and was taking an endless stream of photos, only pausing to post a few online. And the boat hadn't even left the canal's edge yet.

Lana observed in amazement as the younger woman typed out a photo comment using only her thumbs. She looked at her own digits, wondering how Hadley had gotten hers to be so flexible. As she watched the younger woman, Lana realized that in most photos, Hadley positioned her arm so that her multitudes of bracelets were visible.

"I hope you enjoy the cruise," Lana said as she placed cups with hot water and a box of tea bags onto the table. Both Hadley and Tammy nodded in acknowledgement, but otherwise ignored her.

As she poured the last round of drinks, the captain gently steered the boat out into the middle of the canal. Their watercraft eased into an endless stream of similar boats cruising along the same waterway, though Lana noted that most of the other boats were packed full of tourists.

Lana navigated her way back to Gillian, Dotty, and Sally, taking care not to spill the beverages.

As soon as she sat down, Dotty asked, "What was all that fuss about back at the lobby?"

"One of the guests isn't happy with her room."

"I gathered that much. I couldn't see who was complaining. Was it Tammy, by chance? Her daughter already warned me that her mom expected to be treated like royalty. I guess she wasn't joking around."

"Yes, the front desk receptionist said they were Tammy and Hadley Peters. It's the two sitting behind Randy's table." Lana pointed discreetly to the guests in question.

"Ah yes, Tammy and Hadley. The mother had booked a different trip with us last year but got laid off before she could make the final payment. I did refund her money and recommended a less expensive tour company, but she wasn't having it. She had her heart set on a Wanderlust tour, bless her."

"It was kind of you to refund her money. Losing your job unexpectedly does make any vacation an extravagant luxury."

"I know you and Randy got off to a rough start with her, but why don't we play along for the rest of the trip? Most of our guests can afford to go abroad once or twice a year, but she's been saving for a long time to be here."

Lana stared at Dotty and saw only sincerity in her expression. The older lady surprised her constantly with her kindness. "Of course. I'll talk to Randy, but I'm certain he'll be happy to play along."

"Excellent." Dotty slapped the table, getting Gillian's attention. "So, Gillian, I have been looking forward to meeting you. Tell me, do you have a boyfriend?"

Lana's mouth flew open. What was Dotty doing asking Gillian something so personal? Lana paled, hoping her boss was not trying to play matchmaker for her mom.

To Lana's surprise, Gillian nodded slightly.

"I had no idea you were dating," Lana said.

"I wasn't sure how you would react." Gillian said, unable to meet her daughter's gaze.

"It's been twenty years since Dad died…"

"Barry and I have been seeing each other for four years. We've recently started talking about moving in together."

"That's wonderful! I'm happy for you."

"Really?" When Gillian faced her daughter, she seemed truly shocked by Lana's approval.

"Why wouldn't I be? Everyone deserves to be happy."

"Are you, um, seeing anyone?" Gillian asked carefully. Her mother had not approved of Lana's former husband, Ron, and had only come to their wedding to save face with the many family friends in attendance.

Dotty and Sally leaned forward to hear Lana better.

"I am dating, but I haven't met anyone special yet. Despite Dotty's best efforts," Lana added with a smile as she covered Dotty's hand with her own.

"Lana sure is particular. I've gone through my best suitors already but am always on the lookout for more," Dotty teased.

As Lana relaxed into her comfortable banter with Dotty, she noted that her mother's eyes were narrowing to slits. *Was Gillian actually jealous?* Lana wondered.

"When the time is right, it will happen," Gillian said and patted Lana's shoulder.

Lana's eyes widened to saucers. That was the first physical contact they had had in years.

Sally set her purse on the table and took out a ball of yarn.

"Why don't you leave that in your bag for now," Dotty said. "We won't be on the boat long, and the architecture along the canals is quite beautiful."

"You're right; when I knit, I don't sightsee," Sally said.

Gillian rolled her eyes, but Sally didn't appear to notice. She was too busy rummaging around in her bag. Moments later, she pulled out a camera. "I did promise my boyfriend that I would take lots of pictures. I better get started."

"Great idea, Sally," Dotty said, then turned to Gillian. "Lana tells me you own an advertising agency."

Gillian nodded in response.

"How exciting. Isn't running your own company the best? I wouldn't trade the freedom or control for the world."

Gillian relaxed visibly. "Yes it is. Since Lana's father passed, I've made the company my own. I forgot that you are the owner of Wanderlust Tours. Did you inherit it?"

Lana bristled at Gillian's snide remark, feeling protective of Dotty. "No, she worked long hours to build it up into a success," Lana responded before Dotty could. "She also owns several properties and created a clothing line for dogs last year."

Lana swore she saw a glimmer of respect in her mother's eyes when she said, "You are quite the entrepreneur."

"Yes, well, without dedicated employees such as Sally and Lana, I wouldn't get far. I sure am lucky to have found Lana. You raised a daughter with a good head on her shoulders; you should be proud."

Gillian's forehead crinkled.

Lana reddened in shame. Since she had been fired from the newspaper, all of their sporadic conversations had ended with Gillian berating Lana for taking jobs that didn't fulfill her potential.

Feeling confused and hurt, Lana rose from her chair. "Speaking of which, Randy and I better give the introduction spiel before we dock. It is a short cruise."

She headed over to Randy without glancing back. Since he was technically the lead guide on this tour, she wasn't certain whether he wanted to give the speech. After quickly conferring, Lana cleared her throat and began.

"Welcome to the Netherlands! Randy and I are so glad you are able to join us for this fantastic trip through Holland."

"Excuse me, it's not Holland," Tammy interrupted.

Lana's smile wavered. "Sorry?"

"Holland is a province. The country is called the Netherlands."

"You're right. Thanks for correcting me." Lana bowed her head to Tammy, who was clearly quite pleased with herself. Her daughter nodded in approval before she resumed photographing everything in sight.

"After our cruise through the canals, we are going to stop for a high tea at the Museum of Bags and Purses. I hope everyone is hungry because the menu sounds spectacular. Afterwards, we will have a chance to visit the museum and its award-winning gift shop. We will then walk through the Floating Flower Market on our way back to the hotel. You will have two hours to relax and unwind before we meet again in the lobby at 7 p.m. Tonight we have reservations at one of the city's best Indonesian restaurants, Kantjil & de Tijger, where we will be enjoying one of their fabulous rice table menus."

"Boy, you sure are keeping us busy," Frieda called out.

"Yes we are! There are so many wonderful places to see and visit here, and we didn't want you to miss anything. The itinerary is quite full, but we have built in two free afternoons to give you time to unwind or explore Amsterdam on your own. We will also be visiting De Haar Castle, Alkmaar's Cheese Market, the village of Giethoorn, and the Keukenhof Gardens."

Lana paused to let her words sink in before adding, "To be clear, no one is required to go on all of the day trips. Please let me or Randy know if you would rather not join in a tour, so we can make other arrangements for your transportation."

"We paid for all of it, so expect to see Hadley and me on every trip," Tammy announced.

"Excellent, that's the spirit," Lana said, then discreetly glanced at her watch.

"It looks like we will be docking in a few minutes. The Museum of Bags and Purses has a special dining area that is quite spectacular. I think you will be pleased," Lana said, her voice filled with confidence.

Her guests responded with happy sighs. Lana was glad to hear them and she hoped the pictures on the museum's website were up-to-date.

As they rounded the next bend, Dotty pointed excitedly outside towards a narrow canal house squeezed in between two normal-looking ones. The tiny house's façade was only slightly wider than its front door, yet it was five stories tall. "Folks, on your right is one of the smallest homes in Amsterdam. In the seventeenth century, property taxes were determined by the width of a home, which is why so many are quite narrow yet several stories tall."

"Would you look at that?" Frieda said. "I certainly wouldn't be able to live there; I could barely squeeze through the front door!"

"Oh, in case any of you recognized her voice," Lana said while pointing to her boss, "the owner of Wanderlust Tours is joining us! So Randy and I will be on our best behavior." When she winked, most of group laughed along with her.

After Lana rejoined her table, she leaned over to her boss and whispered, "Dotty, before we dock, can you tell me anything else about the guests? I take it they are all mothers and daughters."

"Almost all of them, except the three at the end," Dotty responded softly, nodding towards the trio sitting at the back of the boat. Lana was always surprised at how much information clients shared about themselves when booking a tour. Dotty asked her travel agents to make notes of everything they said, so she could share it with the guides.

"The mother and daughter, Priscilla and Daphne, were the first to book this trip. Then last week, Priscilla called and asked to add another woman, Paige, to the tour. She's a biographer ghostwriting a book about Priscilla's life. Apparently Priscilla was one of the first women to run a Top 500 corporation."

"That's impressive," Lana said.

"Really?" Gillian looked towards the table with interest, then instantly turned white. "That's a horrible coincidence," she muttered.

"What's wrong, Mom?"

"My ad agency ran a marketing campaign for the company that woman was chairman of," Gillian softly replied.

Lana frowned. "Oh, that's too bad. I hope she realizes this is your vacation and won't want to talk shop the whole time."

"Me, too. It was quite a while ago; hopefully she'll have forgotten me," Gillian muttered in response before chewing on her lip.

Lana was baffled by her mother's nervousness. Gillian never mumbled or seemed unsure. In fact, she was one of the most confident women Lana had ever met. If Priscilla was capable of doing this to her mother, Lana would have to get to know her better.

6

Combining Work With Pleasure

When their boat pulled up to the Museum of Bags and Purses, several guests squealed in delight.

"Well, isn't that pretty!" Sara exclaimed.

Lana had read online that the museum was housed in a seventeenth-century canal house, but in person it was even more charming than in the photos. She looked up in awe, hoping the interior was still original.

Her hopes were momentarily dashed when they squeezed into the shockingly modern entrance. Lana's heart sank, fearing her mother was right. Most of the space was filled with bags and purses of every kind imaginable. Once she had confirmed their reservation, an employee pointed them towards another door that led to the museum and café.

Crossing through that doorway was akin to stepping back in time. The old canal house was beautifully restored. The walls were covered with darkly tinted wooden paneling. The railings were extensively carved and felt wonderfully smooth under her hand. The many bags, purses, fans, and jewelry were worked naturally into the delightful interior, displayed as if their wealthy owner had just stepped away to powder their nose. Lana was not and never had been a girly-girl, but even she enjoyed seeing all of the designer bags on display, some as intricate and well-made as any other sort of artwork she had seen.

They climbed up a flight of stairs and were greeted by a waitress who

28

showed them to their table. Gillian's dismissals were immediately forgotten once they stepped into the formal dining room. If anything, Lana felt horribly underdressed. The ceilings were painted with glorious frescoes. Several long tables were decked out in fancy tablecloths, porcelain plates, and crystal water glasses. White decorative molding contrasted well with the intricate wallpaper and velvety curtains. It was a joy just to be here. Lana couldn't wait to sample their lunch.

A waitress explained to the group which foods and teas they would be enjoying during the two-course meal. It all sounded scrumptious. Her group oohed and aahed in delight, clearly captivated by the menu, interior decorations, luxurious draperies, and the tall windows perfectly framing their views of the Herengracht below.

Priscilla, Daphne, and Paige—in Lana's mind, the Group of Three—took seats at one end of the long table. Tammy and Hadley sat next to them, leaving one empty chair in between. Tammy seemed to be impressed with the dining room, smiling for the first time when the waitress snapped open a cloth napkin and laid it in her lap.

Frieda, Sara, and Anne sat on the opposite side, excitedly whispering about the moldings and paintings decorating the ceilings. Based on their expressions, they were satisfied, as well.

Even Gillian seemed to be happy with the location. After she sat down next to Hadley, Dotty and Sally filled in the seats next to her.

"I thought Lana was going to sit there," she said to Dotty, who had just settled herself in the chair on Gillian's left.

Dotty started to rise, her cheeks going red as she did, when Lana intervened.

"If you don't mind, I would prefer to sit on the other end, so I can chat with the guests I haven't spoken to yet. I am working, Mom," Lana said as politely as she could, while placing significant emphasis on the last sentence.

Dotty's forehead crinkled, but Gillian nodded in acknowledgement. After a moment's hesitation, her mother said, "Dotty, do you have a marketing campaign in place for Wanderlust Tours?"

Lana's eyebrows shot up. Gillian strong-arming Dotty into hiring her ad agency was all she needed. *Then again, Dotty is the one who invited her along without even asking me,* Lana thought, *it serves her right.*

Randy stepped close to Lana. "What do you think, should we help the waiters serve everyone?"

Lana looked at the other tables in the dining area, also filled with large groups of middle-aged women. "The waitresses seem to have their routine down pat. We aren't the only big group. I think we can sit with our clients, at least for now."

Randy nodded, then sat at one of the empty chairs situated between Paige and Tammy. Lana took the last free chair, sitting between Frieda and Priscilla.

Lana turned to the Group of Three. Both of the younger women appeared to be in their late twenties. The dark-haired woman, with her thin lips, narrow face, and lengthy body, clearly took after her mother. The second woman—the writer, Lana assumed—had blonde hair, a heart-shaped face, and short stature.

"Hello, I haven't had a chance to introduce myself properly. I am Lana, and I understand you are Priscilla, Paige, and Daphne. It's good to meet you. What do you think of Amsterdam so far?"

"It's really pretty," the blonde said. "I still can't believe we saw so much of the city in just an hour. Amsterdam is tiny! It's nothing like New York."

"Yes, well, New York is three times larger," Priscilla said, wincing at the younger woman's enthusiasm. "I am looking forward to vacationing somewhere quieter for a change, especially with all the work we need to do."

"Oh, I didn't realize you had to work during this trip," Lana said. "Which days do you need to leave the tour? Will your daughter be staying or going with you?" Lana looked to the dark-haired woman.

Priscilla looked at Lana as if she was crazy. "This is my daughter, Daphne." When she pointed at the blonde, Lana had trouble keeping her mouth from gaping open.

"This is Paige." Priscilla gestured towards the dark-haired woman. "She's the reason why I have to work. She is writing my biography," she added in a loud whisper, her eyes twinkling.

Paige held out her hand to Lana. "It's great to meet a fellow writer."

Lana stiffened, wondering what Paige was referring to. All the articles she wrote for her Travel Time blog were anonymous, and she never posted images of herself on the site. She had even created a separate email address and profile to ensure no one from her old newspaper, the *Seattle Chronicle*, discovered what she was doing. A horrible thought entered Lana's brain. Did Paige mean Lana's work as a journalist? Had she somehow found out about Lana's past and the libel lawsuit? Whichever she meant, Paige's remark made Lana wary.

Lana took the writer's hand, albeit limply, as she tried to find her tongue. "Oh, so you aren't family? Gosh, the physical resemblance between you two is quite strong."

Now that Lana knew they weren't related, she could see the differences in their facial features. Paige's nose was shorter and wider, and Priscilla's cheekbones were much more pronounced, but the general similarities were uncanny.

Paige began to glow in response to Lana's remarks, but Priscilla looked as if she had bit a lemon. "What? No, you should get your eyes checked. And no, I won't need to leave the tour to work. Paige will be interviewing me during our free time. I don't think it will intrude on the other guests' enjoyment, but we will try to keep out of your way."

"And during the day trips—of course, as long as it doesn't bother the others, Lana," Paige said, acting as if they were old friends. Something about her chummy tone and demeanor made Lana nervous.

"That sounds like a great way to combine work with pleasure," she responded as casually as she could.

"It really is."

"May I ask why Paige is writing about you?"

"I was the first woman to lead a rather successful Top 500 corporation. I don't want to say which one; too many people have a preconceived opinion about our products. Having a publisher interested in printing a biography about me is quite flattering, but not really unexpected. I have had so many interesting experiences as a woman at the top that there is a lot to share, though sometimes it is hard to dredge up old memories. Especially since they seem to want to know everything about my early years," Priscilla said, glaring at the biographer.

"The series is called The Person Behind the Success. Part of my assignment is to document your past so our readers better understand the people and experiences that shaped you," Paige explained.

"It wasn't my parents or childhood, I guarantee you that," Priscilla said. "I invited Paige to join us because the publisher wants the book out as soon as possible. I'm happy to oblige but don't see the reason for rushing. Even though I retired six months ago, I hardly think potential readers will forget about me so quickly," she laughed.

The woman has a rock-solid ego, Lana thought. "What an incredible opportunity," she enthused. "It's a pleasure to have you on the trip. Have you been to the Netherlands before?"

"No. Daphne booked this trip for us as a retirement present. The Netherlands has always been on my bucket list, but with my hectic schedule, getting away for two weeks was impossible," Priscilla said, beaming at her daughter. Lana still couldn't see any familial resemblance, but she was touched by the young woman's gesture.

"I loved my job, but retirement is proving to be pretty nice, as well. I never did have time to take real vacations when I was at the helm. Too many people relied on my opinion and leadership. It's been good to take a step back and see more of the world. Daphne's convinced me to visit Asia next, isn't that right?"

"China is one of the world's superpowers. I think it's important to know more about it and the neighboring countries," Daphne added. "That's why I've been learning Chinese."

"And you're doing quite well. It is such a tough language to master. I'm in awe of Daphne's drive. I didn't think she had it in her," Priscilla chuckled. Her tone was so condescending that Lana felt bad for Daphne.

A dark cloud crossed over Daphne's face. She stood up and laid her napkin on her chair. "Excuse me."

When Daphne walked away without further explanation, Priscilla called out, "Where are you going?"

32

"The ladies," Daphne responded without looking back. She crossed paths with three waitresses holding large porcelain teapots in their hands. The women approached their table and began pouring tea into their dainty cups while one explained what they were about to drink.

"We will start off with a light jasmine tea, to help cleanse the palate. In a moment, we will bring out the first course."

Lana sat back, listening to the waitress describe the teas' aroma and healing properties while thinking about Gillian's reaction to Priscilla's presence on this tour. The former CEO seems incredibly self-assured, determined, and a born leader—exactly the kind of person Gillian would normally gravitate towards. So why was her mother avoiding Priscilla?

Perhaps their egos clashed when Priscilla was a client, Lana thought. Both women were strong-willed and quite successful in their own right. She would have to pay more attention to what Priscilla told Paige, and see whether she shared any stories about Gillian's advertising agency. Based on Gillian's eagerness to avoid Priscilla, Lana wouldn't be surprised if the recollections were less than favorable.

7

A High Tea Fit for a Queen

As soon as the waiters finished placing their food and drinks on the table, Anne leaned over her mother to ask Lana where the bathrooms were.

"I saw a sign for them by the staircase. Do you want help finding them?" Lana asked.

Sara was already pushing back her chair. "I can go with you, dear."

"It's okay, Mom, I'm not totally helpless."

"That's news to me," Sara grumbled as Anne exited the dining room.

"So, ladies, it doesn't feel right calling you the Fabulous Five this time, considering the others aren't here. Have you thought of a suitable alternative?" Lana joked, trying to lighten the mood.

Frieda took her seriously. "I've been considering the options. Once Franny arrives, there will be four of us. The Fabulous Four is too easy. What about the Fantastic Four?"

"I like it," Sara said, nodding as she rolled the name over her tongue.

Lana started to say that it was already taken by a group of superheroes but decided to go with the flow instead.

"Good. We'll go with that," Frieda stated, closing the subject. "Now, enough talking, it's time to eat this scrumptious meal."

"Oh my, everything looks wonderful," Lana said, while taking in the bite-size sandwiches and pastry rolls. "Which one are you going to try first, Frieda?" Lana nodded her head towards the three-tiered tray of goodies placed between them.

"That sausage roll is calling my name," Frieda said as she grabbed a flaky pastry off the tray.

Lana picked up a salmon sandwich and took a bite. The thinly cut layers of fish and capers melted in her mouth. "Oh, Frieda, Dotty said your daughter is going to join us later. Why didn't she fly over with you?"

"She has to work," Frieda said gruffly. "She's supposed to be flying in from Milan late tonight. We'll see if she makes it."

Sara startled at the name. "Gosh, I haven't seen Franny in ages. She's so darn busy, I'm glad she can join us at all. Is she still –"

"Yes," Frieda hissed. Her jaw was clenched so tight, Lana was afraid it might snap. "She's still prancing around on stage. That girl has such a good head on her shoulders; it's a terrible waste."

Lana raised an eyebrow and opened her mouth to ask what Franny did for a living when Sara shook her head slightly, silencing her.

"At least your daughter is actually doing something with her life," Sara complained. "Since Anne's business ran into trouble, she's been moping around my house instead of working. At this rate, she'll never find enough new clients to resuscitate her business."

Frieda finished her pastry roll and grabbed a cucumber sandwich off the tray. "What happened?"

"Her biggest client decided to cut costs the last time they renegotiated their contract with Anne's cleaning company. Apparently they were reviewing all of their contracts with external vendors, so she shouldn't take it personally, but it was an unexpected blow."

Sara looked to Lana and explained, "Her employees cleaned the company's headquarters. It's a massive building, and she had to hire extra employees to fulfill the contract in the first place."

She turned back to Frieda. "Another cleaning company submitted a lower bid, and Anne either had to match them or lose out. Yet the money they were offering would not have covered her personnel costs and supplies. She couldn't afford to say yes, so they signed with the cheaper competition."

"That's unbelievable! What's happened to loyalty these days?" Frieda moaned in sympathy.

"I swear there is none. She worked so hard to keep them happy for the past ten years, and then they toss her aside, without a single thought for her fifty employees or their families. Since then, she's not been able to sign enough new clients to keep everyone working. If something doesn't change soon, she'll have to lay off more of her staff. McGruffin Wood is one of the state's largest employers. It's going to take several cleaning contracts to equal the work she was doing for them."

Lana's eyes squeezed shut as she gripped the table for support. She hadn't heard that name spoken aloud since the *Seattle Chronicle* lost the libel lawsuit and she her job. "Did you say McGruffin Wood?"

"Yes." Sara looked at her quizzically. "You look like you've seen a ghost. Why, have you had their executives on your tour?"

"Not that I know of. I just haven't heard that name in quite a while," Lana said, keeping her tone neutral. The last thing she wanted to do was have to explain in detail how McGruffin's legal team had made mincemeat of her research into the company's bribery practices and environmental pollution.

"You must not read the local newspapers much anymore. They own most of the state, and their new CEO is going green. It seems like they are announcing a new solar or wind project each week, and they are finally cleaning up several stream beds their paper plants contaminated."

How ironic, Lana thought. She'd lost her job because she tried to expose the company's illegal practices, yet it kept polluting even after she was fired. Her investigation and the resulting articles hadn't forced it to take responsibility for the damage it was causing. It was too bad that it had taken ten years, but she was glad the new CEO was finally stepping up to the plate.

Sara turned back to Frieda. "As I was saying, replacing them as a client is going to be hard for Anne anyway, but she's gotten so depressed, she's lost her motivation to get up in the morning."

And her interest in personal hygiene, Lana thought.

"I really hope this trip reminds her that there's a whole world out there waiting to be explored," Sara continued. "Or, at least, that it motivates her to get off my couch."

"At least you see your daughter," Frieda grumbled. "My Franny can't be bothered to fly home every month anymore."

"Why don't you fly out and meet her?"

"She's always busy with work when I do. And when she does have time off, there's a constant circle of people around her all wanting something from her. No, it's easier for both of us if I don't join her."

Lana's curiosity was well and truly piqued. Was Franny an actress or dancer? Or some sort of motivational speaker? As much as she wanted to ask, Sara's shake of the head made clear that it was better if she did not. Based on both women's reactions, Franny was a subject that made even Sara tread lightly. After the high tea, Lana would have to pull Sara aside and ask her about Franny, in private.

8

Museum of Bags and Purses

"What about you?" Frieda asked as she looked across the table. "It's Gillian, correct? You are Lana's mother, aren't you? I bet you live in Seattle, too."

"Yes, I am, and I do," Gillian said, smiling at Lana as she spoke.

"You're lucky. At least Lana comes back to Seattle between tours so you can catch up."

Gillian blushed and took a sip of her drink. Lana couldn't bring herself to admit the truth, that neither one of them made time for the other, despite the fact that they lived only a few minutes' drive from each other. Instead, she fibbed to save them both the frustrations of having a guest try to "help" them improve their relationship.

"It is pretty special that Mom was able to join us on this Mother's Day trip," Lana responded.

Gillian's eyes momentarily narrowed until she realized Lana was being sincere. "Yes, it is. Say, what do we have planned for Mother's Day, anyway?"

Lana mentally reviewed their trip itinerary. "We will be visiting De Haar Castle that day and having a special luncheon in an old tavern afterwards."

"That sounds fascinating," Gillian said.

"I don't know, castles always give me the creeps," Frieda said.

"This one looks pretty spectacular, Frieda, at least from the photos I found online," Sara said.

Before Lana could regurgitate all that she could remember about the castle,

Anne returned.

"Oh, Anne, it's good you didn't take much longer. We would have eaten it all. I have no self-control when the food is this delicious," Sara said as she licked her fingers.

Sara's comment made Priscilla noticed that her daughter had not yet returned. "Where is Daphne? She's missing the meal."

"I think she is in the ladies' room," Lana offered.

"That was ages ago." Priscilla stretched her neck and searched the room. Lana stood up. "I'll go take a look."

Priscilla nodded and took a sip of her tea.

Lana checked the toilet first. As soon as she entered, she could hear Daphne talking in one of the stalls. She raised her hand to knock but thought better of it. As she turned to leave, the bathroom door slammed open.

Priscilla stormed in, listened for a moment, then screeched, "Are you talking to that deadbeat again? Hang up this instant!" She began pounding on the stall door so hard, Lana was afraid the wood would crack.

Lana stared in disbelief as Daphne opened up, her head hung low.

Priscilla snatched the phone out of her hand before Daphne could react. "I'll hang onto this. You obviously can't be trusted."

"Hey, that's mine. You have no right!"

"I have every right. I pay for everything, including your salary, don't I? Technically, it's mine anyway."

"I'm not a kid anymore. You can't decide who I date," Daphne huffed as she tried to grab her telephone out of her mother's hands. Priscilla dangled it above her daughter's head as Daphne sprung up in an attempt to grab it.

Lana felt so embarrassed for the young woman, she wanted to disappear.

"I refuse to allow you to marry that trash. You keep this up and I will make certain that you get nothing!"

Daphne stormed out of the room without acknowledging Lana's presence. Seconds later, Priscilla did the same.

Lana stood with her back to the stall door, wondering what the heck had just happened. She and Gillian had many issues to work through, but her mother had thankfully never humiliated her in front of strangers before, at least not like this. She took a deep breath, then pushed the bathroom door open and rejoined her group.

When she returned to the table, the women were sitting next to each other again. Daphne stared straight ahead, her mouth set in a firm line. Priscilla was turned to the biographer, enthusiastically answering Paige's questions as if nothing had happened.

Moments later, the second round of food arrived. Two waitresses set tiered trays on their tables as another described the tiny desserts placed onto lacy doilies as macarons, brownies, and apple pie. Soon, a fourth waitress added trays of scones, clotted cream, marmalade, and raspberry jam to the table.

Her guests needed no encouragement to dig in. Based on the groans of delight, Lana was not the only one enjoying her meal.

By the time her group finished every single delicious bite, Lana was so full she was afraid her stomach might explode. Luckily their guided tour of the three-story museum would give them all a chance to walk off their meal.

* * *

Three grand, yet steep, staircases wound their way up the middle of the beautifully restored canal house. Their guide started the tour at the top, in the attic, where the history of bags and purses was explained. The displays showcasing embroidered tie pockets and antique bridal bags were fascinating. Many of the bags were so intricately woven or sown together, they were miniature works of art. When she glanced at her guests, she was glad to see they seemed to be as captivated as she was. Well, all except the Group of Three. Priscilla had decided to stay in the café and work with Paige and Daphne on her book, instead of joining the guided tour.

Too soon, their guide walked them down to the second floor. Lana trailed behind her group, while Randy led the front. As they descended, Tammy sidled up to Sara and asked conspiratorially, "Did I hear you mention

McGruffin Wood?"

"Yes."

"Did they screw you over, too?" Tammy asked.

"Pardon?" Sara asked, clearly offended by Tammy's word choice.

"That CEO, E.P. Andersen, destroyed my life. She cheated me out of my thirty-year bonus by making me redundant."

"That is despicable," Frieda piped up.

"It truly is. I turned down several other job offers to stay with them, and they tossed me aside like a sack of dirt when they didn't need me anymore. With my seniority, it would have been equivalent to a year's salary!"

Lana couldn't believe it. Another victim of McGruffin Wood was on the trip. She momentarily thought it might be a conspiracy, until she reminded herself that McGruffin was one of the state's biggest employers. The odds that two of her guests once worked there was relatively large, when she thought about it. The company did own several wood processing plants, paper mills, and warehouses spread across Washington state.

She didn't recognize the name E.P. Andersen, but knew that she wasn't the CEO when Lana wrote the articles about the environmental pollution McGruffin was causing. Andersen must have been appointed after her predecessor was forced out shortly after the lawsuit was settled, which was the only saving grace in the whole mess, as far as Lana was concerned.

"I convinced my boss to appeal the case, and he discussed it with his superiors. Apparently the board of directors was willing to consider it, but Andersen wouldn't budge. No exceptions would be made to her policy because it would cost the company too much. Three months after they got rid of me, McGruffin announced a record profit for the previous year," Tammy explained, spitting out of anger.

"Soulless, that's what she is," Sara exclaimed. "That horrible woman has no consideration for others."

"If I ever meet that woman, I swear I will throttle her with my bare hands," Tammy said. "That kind of person doesn't understand the sacrifices most people have to make just to survive."

Randy called up to them from the second-floor landing. "Ladies, are you going to join us?"

Lana blushed, embarrassed she hadn't noticed that the rest were already a flight lower. They rushed to catch up, then turned their attention back to the guide. This room showed the evolution of luggage—from classic steamer trunks to rollaway bags—and that of children's school bags. Display cases lining the walls contained small, modern, and contemporary purses that were unique qua design. Several had been donated by famous designers and celebrities, including Gucci, Chanel, Louis Vuitton, Ralph Lauren, Christian Dior, and Paloma Picasso.

Lana half listened as their guide recounted the history of some of the more spectacular donations, including a feather and beads bag by Steve McQueen and a green, ivy-covered clutch by Versace that Madonna had taken to the London premiere of *Evita*. Lana's personal favorite was the Kiss Clutch, a small bag shaped like a pair of bright red lips that had been inspired by Salvador Dali's famous lips couch.

Despite the interesting stories, Lana couldn't stop turning over all of the connections to McGruffin in her mind. She had spent the past ten years of her life trying to forget about her investigation into the company, the resulting libel lawsuit, and McGruffin's eventual escape from punishment for the environmental pollution it had caused. And now she was surrounded by more of its victims.

Their guide ushered them into the next room, breaking her train of thought. She pushed the lawsuit out of her mind and focused on the tour.

After their guide showed them the temporary exhibition of delicate, painted fans and wished them a pleasant day, Lana gathered the group back together.

"Wasn't that incredible?" she asked, smiling at her guests as she listened to their enthusiastic responses. Lana hadn't been a fan of purses when they entered, but by the time they finished their guided tour, even she found the museum to be wonderful and well worth visiting.

"Those early school boxes are incredible. I thought kids had it bad now; they must have had arms of steel to carry those wooden ones around."

"I love that lips purse! I don't know who Salvador Dali is, but those lips were the perfect background for my bracelets. Those photos are going to get me a lot of likes on Instagram," Hadley said.

"I do hope we have time to look in their shop before we go," Sara said.

Lana checked her watch. "We have about a half hour before we walk to the flower market. Does anyone else want to check out their shop before we leave?"

A chorus of enthusiastic affirmations greeted her in response. Lana chuckled. "Well then, follow me."

The museum's shop was filled with an incredible selection of high-end bags and purses, showcasing some of the hottest design talents in Europe. It was a treat to touch the soft leather, explore the multitude of tiny compartments, and marvel at the variety of sizes and shapes. Lana's favorites were the two-toned bags made from the softest leather she had ever felt. However, she set her first choice back on the shelf when she converted the price in her head and realized it would cost her almost five hundred dollars.

"What do you think, Sara, does the blue one or red one suit me better?" Frieda asked, holding a small clutch up to either side of her body.

Sara studied them critically. "I surely don't know. They both look good."

"The red one is infinitely better," Tammy piped up. "It brings out the highlights in your hair. The blue one makes your skin look gray."

Frieda turned to Tammy, and Lana held her breath, expecting a blowout. Tammy hadn't exactly been making friends with the others on the tour. However, the smile on Frieda's face would have made a pearl jealous.

"The red one it is! Thank you, Tammy, I would have hated to waste three hundred euro on a bag that made me look older than I already am."

Frieda pulled Tammy in for a spontaneous bear hug. The grumpy woman looked shocked for a second, before settling into Frieda's embrace. Lana swore she saw the start of a smile forming on her face. *Sometimes all a blusterous bully needs is a hug or kind word*, she thought, making a mental note to compliment Tammy whenever possible.

Lana's eyes swept the shop as she visually checked in on her guests, all of whom had several bags in hand and were asking each other for advice. Even Gillian was getting into the spirit of things, laughing along with the rest as they took turns with the mirror. *Nothing like a good shopping trip to help women bond*, Lana thought. Suddenly she realized they were three short.

"Oh, no, I forgot about the others," Lana said aloud. The Group of Three was still up in the café. She navigated through the narrow aisles full of shopping ladies to get to Randy. He was standing close to the exit and clearly not in his element.

He grabbed her arm as soon as she was within reach. "Lana, thank goodness. I was afraid of knocking over one of the displays and didn't dare come to you. I want to get a purse for Gloria, but I don't have the faintest idea which one she would prefer."

Lana grinned as she patted his arm. "Don't you worry about a thing. Let me take you over to Dotty. She and the others will have you hooked up in no time."

Randy beamed. "That would be wonderful."

"While they are helping you, I am going to check on Priscilla, Daphne, and Paige. I don't know if they want to join us at the flower market, but we should get the rest of the group over there before it closes."

"Okay, we'll wait for you here."

Lana took Randy over to Dotty and explained his predicament. As expected, the older ladies immediately started grabbing bags of all shapes and shoving them into his face as they asked about Gloria's favorite colors, clothing style, and height. She had to chuckle as he tried his best to answer the rapid-fire questions, flustered and stammering. Randy finally pulled out his phone to show them a picture of his girlfriend, garnering a round of approvals in response. Whatever they chose for him, Gloria was going to love it.

9

No Time to Sightsee

When Lana ascended the staircase back up to the café, she was surprised to see that the Group of Three was busy working. She had half expected to see them reading books or lounging around, figuring they were simply not interested in the tour but too polite to say so. Priscilla was animatedly telling a story, her hands gesturing wildly as her eyes shone bright. Daphne sat back, her lips set in a thin line as she stared off into the distance. Paige leaned forward, recording everything Priscilla said with a pen and notepad.

Lana walked up to their table and waited patiently for Priscilla to finish her answer.

"How can we help you?" Priscilla asked instead. Paige glared at Lana, apparently not pleased with the interruption.

"I hate to disturb you, but we are heading to the Floating Flower Market in a few minutes. Would you like to join us, or do you prefer to stay? This café is open for another hour."

"We'll stay here, thanks. We can take a taxi back to the hotel when we are done."

"It's only three blocks…" Lana said, puzzled.

Priscilla waved her hand dismissively. "I assume Wanderlust Tours will be picking up the taxi's tab?"

"Sure, that's fine. Ask the driver to add it to room 17's tab when you return. Will you be joining us for dinner later? We will be meeting in the lobby at 7 p.m."

"No, Paige and I are covering a lot of ground. I would rather keep going. We'll order room service tonight," Priscilla stated, then turned back to Paige, obviously eager to get back to the interview. Lana felt as if she had been dismissed.

"I booked this trip so we could see Amsterdam together. Now all you want to do is work on this stupid book. We already missed the bag museum; I don't want to miss this dinner as well. The restaurant sounds amazing," Daphne whined, her high-pitched voice grating on Lana's nerves.

"Daphne, it is an enormous honor to have an esteemed publishing house want to write about me. And you are my personal assistant; it is your job to be here in case Paige has questions about documents you have access to," Priscilla explained calmly, clearly not for the first time.

Daphne pushed out her lower lip and looked away.

"Stop acting like a five year old!" Priscilla admonished. "If a major publisher asked to write about you, you would have canceled the trip. Not that you've done anything in your life to warrant a book. Without my guidance, you would probably be waiting tables. I told you we would go on the day trips, starting tomorrow," Priscilla said, then turned her attention back to Paige. "Now, where were we?"

Daphne crumpled into her chair.

Paige ignored the outburst and Lana, instead firing off her next question. "I see your company has sued several newspapers for libel. Was there one case that stuck out in your mind?" Her pen hovered above her notebook.

Lana could feel a wave of bile rising in her throat. Simply thinking about the libel lawsuit she had gone through made her physically sick. She had never met the CEO of McGruffin Wood in person; he had refused to meet with Lana during her investigation for the *Seattle Chronicle* and couldn't be bothered to come to court during the libel lawsuit. Lana always wondered what she would say to him if she did run into him. Most of all, she wondered whether she would be able to keep her tone civil. She seriously doubted it.

Lana left her guests in the café, Priscilla and Paige locked in conversation while Daphne sulked, and returned to the rest of her group.

10

Floating Flower Market

When Lana returned to the museum's gift shop, her guests were lined up in front of the cash register, all with at least one purse in hand. Frieda had three.

As she approached, Frieda shoved two of them in Lana's face. "I think my Franny is going to love these. She sure does like to wear fashionable clothes, and these should go with anything."

Frieda had picked out two beautiful and stylish purses for her daughter. One was a classic cut made of black leather with a long thin strap. The second was a backpack-style bag made of tiny strips of leather dyed in an explosion of color. It was over-the-top, yet gorgeous. Lana could imagine any woman would love both of them. Frieda's comment reminded her to pull Sara aside later and ask about Franny. Lana couldn't wait to learn more about this mysterious woman.

After everyone had paid for their purchases, Lana and Randy walked their group to the Munt Tower. For Lana, it was love at first sight. It was a simple clock tower rising out of an arched entryway that used to be one of the gates to the city. The clock struck four as they stood beneath. Lana swayed in time with the tinkling bells, chiming out a short tune. Once it had finished, they walked to the other side of the canal to Amsterdam's famous Floating Flower Market.

Considering they were going to see the Keukenhof, Europe's largest flower garden, later in the tour, Lana was surprised Dotty had included this market on the tour as well. But, according to her guidebooks, it was one of the top tourist attractions in the city and only a block from their hotel. It would have been strange not to visit it.

Lana caught up with Dotty and whispered in her ear, "Do you have a preference for where we start? Or do you just let them shop on their own?"

Lana had been on enough tours now to feel comfortable leading a large group. Yet it was somewhat unnerving having her boss along on the trip. Because Lana had not yet been to any of the cities her groups were visiting, she was reliant on her tour notes, travel guides, and friendly hotel receptionists to know where to go. The rest, she filled in as she went.

However, Dotty had been one of the company's most active guides for fifteen years. She had also written most of the itineraries and tour notes for this trip, as well as most of the tours they offered in Europe. Lana could imagine she had her own way of doing things.

"Lana, honey, I'm just along for the ride. As far as I'm concerned, you're doing splendidly. Those five-star reviews mentioning your competence and friendliness weren't lying. What do you think of Lana's abilities, Sally?" Dotty asked her travel companion.

Sally lowered her camera to respond. So far, she hadn't worked on her knitting project, but she had documented pretty much every step the group had taken. Lana wasn't certain who had shot more photos—Sally or Hadley. That girl was also obsessed with her smartphone's camera and sharing everything on social media. Lana figured if she looked back at Sally's and Hadley's photos after this trip, she could literally relive it, step by step.

"Oh, gosh, I think she's doing just fine." Sally smiled briefly at Lana, then resumed her picture taking.

"Thanks, Sally. Let me just go check in with Randy." Lana had already seen on their map that if they walked through the market from this side, once they exited on the other end, their hotel was only a block away. She caught up to Randy and showed him her map.

"Sounds like a good plan," he whispered, then clapped to get their group's attention.

"We have about an hour to explore the shops and buy any souvenirs before we walk back to our hotel. That may sound like a lot of time, but the shops are quite deep and thus larger than they appear from the street. The market is real close to our hotel, so you can easily come back anytime. I do want to mention there is a shop that sells authentic Delft Blue porcelain in the Munt Tower, and another sells holiday ornaments and decorations year-round in the market. It is extremely busy here, and pickpockets are quite active. Be sure to keep your wallet and phone close."

Lana and Randy led their group into the jumble of tourists going every which way. Their tour notes were still up to date; the floating shops were quite deep and full of potted plants, large sacks of bulbs certified for international transport, and masses of souvenirs.

The two guides stayed out on the street as their clients wandered through the shops, touching or discussing pretty much everything inside. Dotty and Sally were laughing together about the silly marijuana leaf magnets and I Love Amsterdam bags. Lana felt a jolt of jealousy as she watched the two friends. Thanks to their age difference, they could have easily been mother and daughter. How Lana wished that she and Gillian could be so comfortable around each other.

Frieda, Anne, and Sara also stuck together, as did Tammy and Hadley. All five were focused on tulip bulbs to take home; the lone sticking point was how many. Only Gillian seemed out of her element as she wandered aimlessly through the aisles.

"If you want to spend time with your mom, go right ahead. Dotty told me you two had a lot to talk through," Randy said.

"What? I wish Dotty would keep her nose out of everyone's problems," Lana huffed.

"She doesn't mean any harm. It's just her way of being helpful. She doesn't have any children, and I can imagine it pains her to see you two not getting along," Randy said.

Lana hung her head and nodded. "You're right. It's just not a great combination, working and trying to reconnect with your estranged mother. It would have been better if Dotty had invited her over for dinner, instead."

"I don't know. I bet it would have taken a lot of dinners before you two really got to talking again. Inviting Gillian on this trip is Dotty's way of throwing you two into the deep end."

"Maybe she should have trusted that we already know how to swim."

11

Truth Time

As Lana stepped out of the shower, she couldn't help but whistle a jaunty tune. After such a long day, it felt good to wash the dirt and sweat off. It wasn't only the feeling of cleanliness that put her in a good mood. Despite her mother's presence on this tour and the full schedule, most of her guests were getting along like old friends. Dotty had spent their dinner regaling everyone with some of her funnier travel-related stories while they dined as royalty at the exclusive Kantjil & de Tijger restaurant. Even Tammy was impressed by the speediness of the wait staff, extensive menu, quality of the dishes, and posh surroundings.

According to Lana's guidebooks, Kantjil & de Tijger was one of the top Indonesian restaurants in Amsterdam. Back in Seattle, Lana ate at Thai, Indian, and Vietnamese restaurants regularly, but she had never tried Indonesian before. Though some dishes were similar to what she was used to, most used different spices and sauces. What was most unusual about their dinner was the way it was served. Instead of each person ordering a single meal, twenty-four different dishes were placed strategically around the table, with servers regularly coming by to help diners reach and sample everything on the menu. It was heavenly. Between the high tea and dinner, Lana had eaten so much food today that she doubted she would have to eat breakfast tomorrow.

Lana towel-dried her dark brown hair, momentarily wishing she was home.

After such a long and intense first day, all she wanted to do was snuggle up with her cat. Since she wasn't in the same city, she did the next best thing. Lana fired up her laptop and called her best friend and temporary cat sitter, Willow Jeffries.

Willow answered the video call on the first ring. "Hello, Lana! How are you doing?"

Her tone was jovial, but Willow looked anything but. Even through the small screen, Lana could tell she was paler than usual, and her eyes were bloodshot.

"Doing better than you," Lana teased, though her voice was laced with concern. "Are you feeling okay?"

"Not really. Jane and I tried a new oyster bar last night, and the shellfish didn't agree with either one of us."

"I'm sorry to hear that."

A blur of black flashed across the screen, then landed on Willow's lap.

Seymour stared into the video screen and meowed "hello."

"Darling Seymour! I so want to cuddle with you right now." Lana resisted the urge to scratch at his chin through the screen.

Seymour arched his back and turned three times before settling into Willow's lap, his eyes locked onto the screen. His purrs of contentment made Lana feel right at home.

"So how is the trip going? What do you think of the Netherlands?"

"Well, we've only seen Amsterdam so far, but it's even cuter than I imagined it would be. The Museum of Bags and Purses was an unexpected hit, and the high tea went well. Everything is so small and compact—the roads, houses, even the cars. And the bicycles! Oh my, I've never seen so many in my whole life."

"That sounds delightful," Willow said, then paused for a beat. "You know, I'm not Dotty. You can tell me the whole truth."

Lana chuckled. Even when ill, Willow saw right through her.

"Dotty invited Gillian along and didn't tell me. Instead, she surprised me at the check-in counter."

"Oh no—Gillian, as in, your mother?" Willow gasped. "How could she do that, without asking first?"

"She was trying to be helpful, but Dotty doesn't know what she's up against. It's partly my own fault; I didn't tell her everything about our relationship because I didn't want her to concern herself with making it better. Years of resentment and hurt feelings don't just disappear overnight."

Willow sighed. "I'm so sorry, Lana. If Dotty had asked, I would have told her it was a terrible idea."

A knock on Lana's door made her head turn. She started to rise, wondering which guest needed assistance, when a familiar voice called out. "Lana, are you in there? We need to talk."

"Speak of the devil." Lana puffed out her cheeks and stared at her ball of fur, curled up on Willow's lap. In the past three months, Lana had led a kayaking and whale-watching tour in Mexico, a bird-watching tour in Costa Rica, a fjords and walking tour in Norway, and city trips to Budapest, Berlin, and Paris. It had been a fantastic whirlwind of faces and places, but it also meant Lana and Seymour had been apart far longer than either was used to. Lana sometimes feared her cat would forget about her—or, worse, prefer another lap to her own.

"Seymour, honey, I wish I could pet you right now."

Her cat stared at the screen with his serene black eyes. The knocking on Lana's door resumed. "I better go. I sure hope you feel better soon, Willow."

"Lots of tea and animal cuddles seem to be doing the trick." Willow smiled weakly. "Good luck with Gillian."

"Thanks, I'm going to need it."

The knocking intensified as Lana hung up. She hurried over to the door. "Hi, Mom, come on in."

Gillian hesitated, as if she was suddenly unsure as to why she had come by. "Alright."

She entered and sat on the edge of the bed.

Lana stood across from her with her arms crossed over her torso. "What can I do for you, Gillian?"

The use of her first name made her mother's eyes widen. "It has been a crazy day, hasn't it?" she said softly.

"Yeah, I guess it has." Lana uncrossed her arms. "So what did you think about the first day of tours?"

"High teas and flowers aren't really what I am interested in," she said dismissively, twisting the edge of her sleeve in her hand.

Lana rolled her eyes and took a step back when Gillian grabbed her arm.

"Lana, wait, I'm sorry. I don't know why I am acting like this. It's been so long, I don't know what to say to you. Dotty tells me you have a blog. Is that true? Are you writing again?" Gillian actually sounded hopeful.

Lana stopped and took a deep breath, determined to not ruin this chance to get to know her mother again. "Yes, I am. It's actually really fun to write again, without the pressure of a deadline or worrying about an editor's approval."

"What do you write about?"

"Travel. Most of my blog posts are about the places we visit on our tours and what tourists can expect to see. It's becoming quite popular."

"That's great! Are you monetizing it effectively?"

"What?" Lana's stomach sank. "Why does everything have to be about money and positioning yourself in the market? I write the articles because it makes me happy."

Gillian sucked in a large lungful of air and nodded. "You're right. What do your old newspaper buddies think of it? Maybe the *Seattle Chronicle* would like to run one of your articles, now and again?"

"Are you kidding me?" Lana shook her head. "We haven't talked in a very long time, Mom. After I got fired, my friends at the paper pretended I didn't exist. No, worse, they told everyone who would listen that I was a liar who tarnished their profession."

Gillian went as white as a sheet. She started to reach out to her daughter, but Lana jerked away.

"I'm so sorry, Lana. I had no idea that they had turned their backs on you."

"Yeah, well, you weren't around either. It was a pretty lonely time."

"We haven't spoken in so long, it's hard to know where to begin," Gillian admitted.

Lana sat down next to her mother.

"Why don't we begin with, why are you really here?" Lana asked gently, determined not to bait her mother with her tone.

"What do you mean? Dotty invited me along, and I thought it would be a great way to reconnect with you."

"Huh, that's almost word for word what Dotty said. I guess what I am trying to find out is why you suddenly want to be part of my life. I've made it through the past ten years without you. I don't believe you're here simply because Dotty called you."

"No, though her timing was serendipitous." Gillian sucked in her cheeks. "Barry and I want to get married. He wants you to come to the wedding and, well, to be a part of our life. I couldn't invite you to the ceremony without knowing how you feel about me first."

Lana's eyes about popped out of her head. "Wait, so you're only here for your boyfriend."

"Of course not. Patching things up with you is the right thing to do."

Lana's laugh was bitter. "Mom, it has taken me years to find friends I trust and rely on. I love them because I can count on them, and they know that I'll be there for them, too. What about you? Do you actually want to get to know me as a person again, or just make sure I'll be civil at your wedding and whenever else Barry wants to get together and pretend to be a family?"

"I told Barry you were stubborn and that coming on this trip was a bad idea."

"Thanks for that shot of encouragement," Lana said, wishing again that Dotty could have left well enough alone. Long ago, Lana would have loved to patch things up with her mom. But after years of feeling pushed aside and ignored, it was difficult to be open and receptive to Gillian's interest.

Gillian shook her head. "I'm sorry. I'm just so nervous, I don't know what to say to you. I can't redo the past ten years. I feel bad that I haven't been involved in your life. Dotty told me a little bit about what you've been going through. I didn't realize how hard you were having it. But I want to be here for you now."

"Maybe instead of coming on this trip, you could have called and said 'hi.' That would have been a better start," Lana said, then instantly regretted it.

"It's a two-way street, Lana," Gillian blurted out, then covered her mouth with her hand.

"Mom, I appreciate you stopping by. But it's been a really long day, and we have another long one tomorrow. I'll see you at breakfast, with the rest of the guests, okay?"

Gillian's mouth gaped open.

Lana felt like such a jerk and knew she was making things between them worse. But the caldron of rejection, jabs, and hurtful remarks swirling around inside her kept Lana from backing down.

She rose and stood next to the door, signaling the end of the conversation.

Gillian walked out in a daze. When she turned to look back, Lana closed the door.

12

Venice of the North

May 3—Day Two of the Wanderlust Tour in Giethoorn

Lana skipped down the stairs to the breakfast bar, hoping her guests were still in good spirits after their first day. Today's trip to Giethoorn, a small village in the north of the Netherlands, would take up most of the morning and afternoon, and she hoped another daylong tour wouldn't wear her group out.

The first person she saw was Daphne, and she was alone again. To Lana's surprise, Daphne had joined them at dinner last night, even though Paige and Priscilla had stayed at the hotel. Unfortunately they had sat at opposite sides of the table, so Lana hadn't had a chance to find out why she had changed her mind.

"Hi, Daphne. What did you think of dinner last night?"

"It was delicious. You could have rolled me back to the hotel, I ended up eating so much." She looked across the breakfast buffet and then at her empty plate. "To be honest, I'm still full."

Lana picked up a bowl instead of a plate. "Me, too," she said with a laugh. "A cup of yogurt will be plenty."

"Good idea," Daphne said.

"I'm glad you were able to join us," Lana said. "So you didn't have to work, after all?"

Daphne shrugged. "Paige had more questions about Mom's childhood, so she didn't need me to stay. They're back at it again but should be down in a few minutes. Frankly, I was thrilled to get out of that hotel room. The room is nice enough," Daphne added, apparently worried she had unintentionally insulted Lana, "but this isn't the mother-and-daughter trip I was hoping for."

"Why did Priscilla invite Paige to join you on this trip, instead of waiting two weeks to conduct the interview after you'd returned to Seattle?"

"The publishing house wants to get this book out before the end of the year, which means they need to start the writing process as soon as possible. Though truth be told, I think Mom was so flattered by the proposal that she wanted to impress Paige by inviting her to join us. I don't think Paige was pushing to come."

"I'm sure it is quite flattering to have someone want to write about your life. Did I hear Priscilla correctly—are you her personal assistant?"

Daphne's face clouded over. "Yes, unfortunately I still am."

Daphne must have noticed Lana's puzzled expression. "I have been her assistant for ten years. I thought that after she retired, I would stay with the company and continue my career in marketing. But she seems to think her life still warrants a personal assistant." Daphne's mouth was set in a firm line. Based on her expression, she was not pleased with this turn of events.

"Couldn't you have said no?" Lana asked, immediately regretting putting her guest on the spot. "Sorry, I shouldn't have –"

"No, it's okay. In hindsight, I should have." Daphne grabbed a bowl and turned away from Lana, signaling the end of the conversation.

Lana looked up to see Frieda, Anne, and Sara entering the room. "Good morning, ladies. Did you sleep well?"

"Like a baby," Sara responded.

"How are your rooms?"

"Fantastic! I have a four-post bed—can you believe it? I half expected to see a chamber pot underneath," Frieda gushed.

Lana looked to Anne, but the younger woman kept her eyes on the ground. Her hair was still stringy, and her clothing was quite rumpled. Lana wondered whether she had showered since they arrived. She hoped that Sara was right and that this trip would bring Anne out of her shell. She obviously needed something to kick-start her back into living.

"What about you, Anne? Are you happy with your room?"

"Yeah, it's fine," she mumbled.

"Great, glad to hear it." Lana smiled as brightly as she could, hoping to get a grin out of Anne, but to no avail. *Well, at least she responded to my question. That's better than nothing*, Lana thought.

"Say, where is your daughter, Frieda? Is she still sleeping?" Lana looked around them, expecting to see her client's daughter trailing behind.

"Franny couldn't get a seat on the red-eye, so she's flying in this morning. I'm not entirely certain when she will arrive." From her tone, it was clear that Frieda was not pleased.

"At least she is able to join us today. And if she has not arrived before our bus does, I'll arrange for a taxi to drive her out to Giethoorn."

"She better not miss this tour. Giethoorn is why I wanted to come on this trip," Frieda grumbled.

"Of course. We will all do our best to make sure you can spend the day together. Does anyone want coffee or tea?"

Lana poured coffee for all three ladies, and then for herself. As she replaced the carafe, Hadley and Tammy arrived and immediately headed to the buffet. Both women were wearing long peasant skirts made from a paisley fabric and ruffled burgundy blouses. Hadley had a belt with tiny bells woven into it, which really tied the outfit together. Unfortunately, her arms were again bedecked with those ugly beaded bracelets she favored. She was a pretty girl who obviously spent a lot of time on her appearance, but it was too bad about the jewelry, Lana thought. It just didn't fit with her well-chosen outfit.

Lana greeted her guests, then sat back down next to Frieda. As Hadley and Tammy walked along the extensive breakfast buffet, scooping up a little of everything, the door opened again.

A tall, thin beauty entered and scanned the room. Her long hair seemed to be made of honey and her teeth from pearls. Lana was momentarily in awe of the woman—obviously a photo model—when screams made her turn towards the breakfast buffet.

"It's Francesca! Francesca is staying at our hotel!" Hadley shrieked as she dropped her plate and pulled out her smartphone.

Tammy mumbled, "Who?"

"She's only one of the top models on the circuit right now and was just chosen as a Victoria's Secret Angel," the young woman squealed, oblivious to the fact—or not caring—that the model in question could hear her.

The goddess didn't break stride, but her smile did dim slightly. She kept walking towards the breakfast tables. *Scratch that*, Lana thought, the drop-dead-gorgeous woman was sashaying her way towards *their* table. As she approached, her grin increased again in intensity.

Frieda rose, a frown on her face and disappointment in her voice. "You're late."

The model leaned down, her gold locks cascading over Frieda's shoulders and pulled the older woman into a hug. "It's good to see you, too, Mom."

Lana's mouth dropped open in shock.

As mother and daughter relaxed into each other's arms, the model said, "I'm so sorry I couldn't join you yesterday. The evening flights were full. I got the last seat on this morning's flight."

Frieda pulled back from her embrace and turned to Sara, Anne, and Lana. "Ladies, this is my Franny," she beamed.

"It's been too long," Sara said as she rose and gave the younger woman a hug.

"It's nice to meet you. Your mother is quite a hoot," Lana said, getting a laugh out of the model.

Frieda frowned as she examined her daughter. "Look at you—all skin and bones! Let's get you a plate to eat, okay?"

"Oh, Mom," Franny chuckled as she threw an arm over her mother's shoulder and walked with Frieda to the breakfast bar.

Lana couldn't help but stare. *Was that Frieda's biological daughter?* she wondered. Moments later she felt something wet on her blouse. She looked to down to see juice flowing out of her tilted glass and onto her clothing. "Shoot," she mumbled, feeling clumsy in the presence of such beauty and grace.

Sara looked over at Lana and nodded at her wet blouse. "I thought it was better for you to meet Franny in person than for me to try to explain everything."

13

Sailing Through Giethoorn

The two-hour bus ride to Giethoorn was more exciting than Lana had expected, in part due to Franny's presence on the tour. Hadley was apparently quite a fan of the model's look and style and spent most of the trip trying to ask her advice and opinion about fashion.

It was clear that neither Frieda nor Franny was pleased with the intrusion and wanted to catch up, not field questions from fans. As their driver was pulling into Giethoorn, Frieda pushed her way up to the front of the bus and crooked a finger at Lana. "I need your help. That Hadley girl won't leave my Franny alone. We're here on vacation. Can you help us keep her away?"

"Of course, I understand completely. I'll do my best," Lana patted her guest's shoulder in a reassuring way. Though she couldn't forbid Hadley from speaking to Franny, she could do her best to keep them separated.

Once everyone exited the bus, Franny and Frieda made a point of hanging back, while Lana went over to Hadley and Tammy and asked about their trip. Lana kept walking and talking, making it impossible for the two to lag behind and pester the model without being rude.

According to their map, it was only three blocks from the parking lot to the boat rental. Randy took the lead, guiding the group as if he knew exactly where he was going and had been here hundreds of times. He was bluffing, of course.

Luckily, Giethoorn was quite small and easy to navigate. Randy led their group to a canal lined with cafés and boat rental shops. Lana was a bit taken aback by the location. The long waterway ran through pasturelands, and the few buildings in sight were all modern. From the pictures Lana had seen, she had expected to see adorable, reed-covered homes as soon as they crossed over the city line.

"There it is," Randy soon called out, pointing to the company they had reserved three boats with. "Okay, gang, I am going to go inside and let them know we are here. I see there is a toilet on the right and benches along the water. Be right back."

As soon as Randy walked away, Dotty said, "Did you know that Giethoorn is one of the cities listed on the international edition of Monopoly?"

Lana and several other guests murmured their surprise. "How the heck did they manage that feat?" Sally asked, as if she was reading Lana's mind.

"They rigged the system," Dotty answered.

"What? How could a tiny Dutch town rig a worldwide election?" Priscilla asked.

"The town printed up flyers encouraging tourists to vote. You wouldn't believe it by looking at it, but more than two hundred thousand tourists come here each year, and most are from Asia. Apparently their request went viral in China, which accounted for a lot of the votes in Giethoorn's favor. And because there was no limit to how often a person could vote, some of the locals voted several times a day, as well."

"That is impressive," Priscilla stated, studying the town with new eyes. "When you consider how small this place is, it is quite a feat."

Randy soon returned with an employee holding three keys. When the man walked over to three flat-bottom, aluminum boats that could easily fit eight passengers, Randy motioned for Lana to join them. She had assumed the boat rental included a skipper. But when the boat's owner started to explain how the motor worked, she realized they were meant to steer the boats themselves.

Randy thanked the owner as he took the three keys, and together he and Lana walked back to their guests. As she approached, Lana heard Priscilla ask her mother, "Do I know you? You look so familiar."

"Is that so?" Gillian turned and pretended to study her. "I am active in a number of charities. We must have met at a function," she said, then looked away.

Priscilla continued examining her. "I usually have such a good memory for faces. What do you do for work?"

Lana looked at her watch, well aware that their two-hour time slots had officially begun. "Sorry to interrupt, ladies, but it appears we get to steer our own boats. Does anyone want to be captain for the day?"

"I don't want to steer, I need to take photos," Hadley whined.

"Well, I'm not steering. That's why we pay you good money," Tammy said dismissively.

"We are NOT sitting in the same boat as those people," Frieda whispered vehemently to Lana while glaring at Tammy and Hadley.

"I tell you what, why don't we split into three groups first. Tammy and Hadley, why don't you ride with Sally and Dotty? Frieda, Franny, Sara, and Anne can ride in the second boat. That leaves Gillian, Priscilla, Daphne, and Paige in the third boat."

"I want to ride with Dotty," Gillian piped up and walked over to Lana's boss. Dotty's eyes widened in surprise.

"I'm happy to steer our boat," Daphne said.

"You can't steer a boat!" Priscilla laughed. "No, Lana, I would prefer it if you drove us." She turned to her daughter. "Lana is a strong, assertive woman. You could learn from her."

Paige seemed bemused by Priscilla's comments. Lana blushed at Priscilla's remark, until she looked at Daphne and noticed the woman's eyes were shooting daggers at her.

"I have a sailing and diving certificate. Why don't you trust me to steer this dinghy?" Daphne asked her mother.

"This isn't a sailboat, is it?" Priscilla pointed out, as she stepped into the watercraft.

While Daphne and Paige joined her, Lana turned to the rest. "Okay, gang, who wants to be captain of your boats?"

"I'm happy to steer ours," Franny offered.

"That would be lovely, thank you, Franny," Sara said, adding, "Could you teach Anne how to steer, as well?"

Her daughter looked as if she wanted to choke her mother. "That's okay, Franny, you don't need to hold my hand."

"It's no problem at all. It's quite easy once you get the hang of it," Franny said jovially.

"Do you want to steer the last boat, Randy?" Lana asked. He had been content to stay at the back and let her split up the groups. He seemed unusually distracted and distant today. Lana hoped he was doing alright. She'd have to pull him aside later and ask what was bothering him.

"Nonsense, I'm driving ours. I don't have my boating license for nothing!" Dotty said.

Randy bowed to their boss. "It would be an honor."

Tammy straightened up, her eyes twinkling as she turned to her daughter. "The owner is going to steer our boat! Now that is what I call service."

After lots of laughter and several near misses, her group was safely on board, and soon they were puttering away in a slow-moving line of boats.

The heart of the village consisted of two long canals that formed a T. Lining both sides were the adorable thatch-roof homes and farms she had been expecting to see. Their boats sailed under the many wooden bridges straddling the canals. Each seemed to be wide enough for two people to cross. Most of the painted bridges were, in fact, entrances to houses on the opposite side of the water and were blocked off with "Private Property" signs.

"Geez, Giethoorn is tiny," Priscilla said.

"Didn't you grow up in a small town?" Paige asked. "What can you tell me about it?"

"That I got out as soon as I could." Priscilla turned to face Paige, irritation etched in her face. "Why do you seem more interested in who I took to the high school prom than my professional life? You haven't even asked about all the takeovers and mergers I led, or any of the cooperative projects I initiated with Japanese and South African companies. In fact, one of my last acts as CEO was merging two underperforming paper mills into one, which not only saved the company millions, it made the resulting mill one of the most profitable. That's the sort of thing I expected you to ask me about."

"Those stories are so well documented; I'm searching for the hidden gems that can't be found in newspapers."

"They are hidden for a reason. Mainly because they aren't important."

Paige looked as if Priscilla had slapped her. "What do you mean? Your actions and choices as a young woman shaped you."

Priscilla laughed. "Not all of them. Some choices are better forgotten. Besides, nothing truly important happened in my life until I became a vice president. Well, except Daphne, of course." Priscilla patted her daughter's knee. Daphne smiled in return, but her eyes weren't in on it.

Paige's eyes narrowed to slits.

Lana was astonished by how seriously the writer was taking her job. But then again, it sounded like they had a tight deadline and a unique concept for a biography.

Priscilla turned to Lana. "What was that misunderstanding on the bus about? I thought I heard Tammy mention McGruffin Wood."

"Yes, she missed out on her full pension because she was laid off. She was just blowing off some steam, I guess. She's not a fan of the corporation." Lana had trouble keeping her tone civil. She was not a fan of their practices or policies, either.

Priscilla's lips pursed, and she gave Lana a tight nod. "Everyone has an opinion."

Lana looked at her quizzically and opened her mouth to ask why she cared when Paige asked, "What is it like being on a tour with your mother?"

Her question caught Lana off-guard. "It is quite different than if we were on vacation together. I don't have as much time to just hang out with her, of course, but it's nice to spend the week with her, especially considering it is Mother's Day. Does your mother live in Seattle?" Lana asked spontaneously.

Paige's expression grew grim. "No, my parents died a few months ago. I mean, my adoptive parents."

"I'm sorry to hear that."

Paige shrugged. "My adoptive parents were alright, but we were never really close." The writer snuck a look at Daphne while she spoke. It seemed to Lana that she was checking Daphne's reaction. However, neither Daphne nor Priscilla seemed interested in what Paige had to say.

"It's tough being adopted and not knowing who your real parents are. It leaves you feeling a bit lost in life," Paige said, her tone growing in irritation as her voice rose. She glared at both Priscilla and Daphne, but they didn't notice.

What an odd situation, Lana thought. Though Paige was technically here on vacation with Priscilla and Daphne, neither woman was interested in learning more about the writer as a person. When Paige wasn't actively asking questions, both women ignored her. And Paige was such a wallflower, it was easy to forget she was present. Yet from the looks of things, Paige was getting fed up with their indifference. Lana felt obligated to chat with the writer.

"Gosh, that must have been difficult for you, growing up with parents you didn't feel close to," Lana said.

Paige pulled a face. "Don't get me wrong, they didn't beat me or anything like that. But I always got the impression that they expected more from me, more than I could give. I guess because I wasn't really theirs."

Paige's emotionless tone broke Lana's heart. "Did you ever consider requesting to see your adoption paperwork? I thought adopted children were allowed to see it, after they turned eighteen."

"I did, but the archives had burned down years earlier, and no digital copies had been made. My adoptive parents refused to help me because they were convinced I would forget about them if I found my real mother. I even hired a private detective, but he wasn't much help."

"That must be rough, not knowing," Lana empathized. How could Paige's adoptive parents be so cruel? If the woman was so desperate to find her biological mother that she hired a detective, why couldn't they have helped her out?

"Yes, well, sometimes answers appear in the most unexpected places. I've since learned that there are worse things than not knowing who your parents are," Paige said.

Her tone was so bitter, Lana thought it best to let the topic rest. She could only imagine how frustrating it must be for her, not knowing who her parents were. Or whether they were still alive.

14

A Late Night Argument

May 3—Day Two of the Wanderlust Tour in Amsterdam

Traffic on the highways ringing Amsterdam was heavier than expected, making their group an hour late for their dinner reservation at the Rijks, a traditional Dutch restaurant located at the foot of the Rijksmuseum. Luckily Lana was able to reach the restaurant by phone, and its staff kindly held their tables longer. It was a wonderful meal of red cabbage soup, scallops, and duck that she would have hated to have missed.

After they got back to the hotel, Lana was ready to take a hot bath before snuggling under the covers. Tomorrow's trip to Zaanse Schans was another all-day tour, and she wanted to get a good night's sleep. If only her guests felt the same way, she mused, listening to voices next door rising in anger. Lana wasn't entirely certain who Priscilla was fighting with, but it was turning into a doozy.

Until they settled down, she wouldn't be able to sleep. Her curiosity got the better of her. Lana threw back the covers, opened her window, and listened, trying to discern what their argument was about. Through Priscilla's open balcony doors, Lana could only understand a few snippets. Whoever she was fighting with, it was a woman, but Lana couldn't be certain whether it was Paige or Daphne. Both women had similarly nasal voices.

Lana was stepping away to the bathroom, when Priscilla's screams drew her back.

"Don't you tell me what I should feel. I lost out on a promotion because of that incident. I would have reached the top faster if it hadn't have happened. At least I learned French," Priscilla said.

Lana heard a loud slap.

"How dare you!" Priscilla erupted. Lana was stunned that someone had dared strike Priscilla.

Priscilla continued speaking but must have walked away from her balcony doors because Lana couldn't understand a word. She leaned out the window, hoping to catch a glimpse of Priscilla's visitor, when Priscilla's booming voice startled her.

"Of course his name is not listed. I didn't want to embarrass him," Priscilla said.

She must be pacing, Lana thought, because her voice was suddenly much louder. The other woman, however, seemed to have moved away from Priscilla. Lana couldn't hear her response, but Priscilla's next comment was crystal clear.

"It was an embarrassment! Why do you think I gave it away?"

"It?" Priscilla's sparring partner shrieked. The pain in her voice was so evident that Lana was suddenly concerned for Priscilla's welfare. She pulled on a bathrobe and had her hand on her doorknob, when she heard Priscilla's door slam shut. She stood stock still, listening, but heard no more voices.

Figuring their argument was resolved for the night, Lana closed her window and turned to her bed. Hopefully whatever that fight was about could be dealt with in the morning.

Before Lana could get a leg in bed, a fist pounded on her door. Wondering who she would find on the other side, Lana opened it slowly. Standing before her was Priscilla, and she was trembling.

"Are you alright?" Lana asked.

"I need to speak to the owner, Dotty Thompson. Which room is she in?"

Lana pointed to their left. "Room 11, six doors down."

Priscilla nodded and stormed off.

Lana watched her guest knock on Dotty's door, then be ushered inside.

Lana began closing her door when a flash of color made her open it again. *What is going on now?* she wondered. Dashing down the hallway was Anne, Sara's daughter. At least, that was Lana's initial impression. When she looked again, Lana blinked in confusion, suddenly unsure whether it was indeed Anne. This woman racing away was all dolled up in skintight, shiny clothes and platform heels. Her hair was teased up with tons of hairspray. When the woman turned in profile, Lana noticed her glasses were gone and she was wearing a thick layer of makeup.

Was that really Anne? If it was, what happened to her frumpy client? Lana shook her head, questioning her vision. Before she could say anything, the woman darted around the corner and out of sight.

15

The Tour Must Go On

May 4—Day Three of the Wanderlust Tour in Amsterdam

After Priscilla's unexpected visit, things quieted down, and Lana was able to get a good night's rest. When someone knocked on Lana's door at seven in the morning, she was lacing up her boots and almost ready to go. Expecting it to be Randy coming to get her, Lana opened the door and grabbed her jacket without looking at her visitor. "Come on in," she called out.

"Lana, thank goodness you're still here," a woman exclaimed.

Lana jumped, startled to hear a female voice. "Sally? What's wrong?"

"Oh, Lana, Dotty is feeling so poorly, I'm afraid we won't be able to join you today."

"Oh, no. What happened?" Lana asked, ushering Sally inside.

"She's going to be okay. We went out for a midnight snack last night and found an all-you-can-eat dim sum restaurant. It sure was delicious, and we definitely got our money's worth, but all that greasy food seems to have messed up Dotty's insides. She can't really leave the hotel room right now, if you know what I mean."

Lana groaned. "A touch of tummy trouble, eh? Does she need a doctor or medicine?"

"I think she just needs to rest and drink a lot of tea to flush all that oily food out of her system."

"Thanks for letting me know, Sally," Lana said. "How are you feeling?"

"I was feeling a little unsure this morning, but my intestines have calmed down, and I'm back to normal now. We did go overboard, but those little egg rolls are so yummy. We couldn't stop ourselves from going back for more. I better see if Dotty needs anything."

"Are you going to stay with her, or do you want to join the day tour?"

"Oh, gosh, I couldn't enjoy Zaanse Schans knowing Dotty was all alone and feeling poorly. She's like a mother to me! No, I'll stay and take care of her."

Lana bit her tongue as a wave of jealousy washed over her. *No, she's like a mother to me*, she thought, then immediately felt guilty. Sally had known Dotty for many years, far longer than Lana had known her. And Dotty was one of those people who loved to mother everyone around her.

"Should I pop by? Or leave her be?" Lana said instead.

"Honestly, she's pretty embarrassed that she's gotten sick. It might be best to let her be for now. Why don't you stop by after your tour of Zaanse Schans? Hopefully she'll be feeling better by then."

"It's a date," Lana said as Randy rounded the corner and waved.

"Are you ready to go, Lana?"

"Just about. Thanks, Sally. I'll see you in a few hours."

Lana grabbed her bag after Sally returned to her patient.

Lana explained Dotty's predicament to Randy while they walked to the breakfast room. To her surprise, they were not the first ones downstairs. Priscilla and Daphne sat at a table towards the back, deep in conversation. Neither reacted to the guides' presence or good morning greetings. Lana and Randy let their guests be and walked to the buffet.

The rest of their clients trickled in slowly, glad to accept Lana's offer of a strong coffee. After their guests were settled, Lana picked up a plate and began scooping up her own breakfast when Paige entered.

The writer crossed the dining room in record time, making a beeline for Priscilla.

"I told you to leave me alone," Priscilla growled.

Paige laughed at her. "You invited me along; I'm not going anywhere. We still have lots of years to cover."

Priscilla looked to her daughter. "Keep her away from me, will you?"

"Do it yourself," Daphne snapped.

Priscilla's eyes narrow. "Watch out or you will be out of a house, job, and inheritance before this trip is over."

Daphne's eyes widened as her mother's threat sunk in. Seconds later, her demeanor changed. "Why won't you stop pestering my mother? We told you repeatedly that her childhood is off limits. I'm calling your publisher as soon as they open and telling them to send over another biographer, one who will treat my mother with respect."

"You can't do that," Paige protested loudly. "And even if you do, they will say no. I am already well underway, and they want to publish this as soon as possible, before people forgot that your mother, E.P. Andersen, was ever CEO of McGruffin Wood. Besides, Priscilla wouldn't want me to tell you about..."

Cutlery and cups crashed onto the tables as Tammy and Anne ran over to Priscilla. "You are E.P. Andersen?" Tammy screeched.

"Her initials stand for Erin Priscilla," Paige explained. "Personally, I like Erin better."

"Do I look like a cheerleader to you?" Priscilla retorted as she rose to her accusers.

"Your decision to close that paper mill ruined so many lives! How can you live with yourself, you greedy cow?" Tammy shrieked.

Before Lana and Randy could intervene, Tammy jumped up onto Priscilla's back and began kicking her sides. Priscilla beat at Tammy's legs with her fists, trying to get her off. It looked like Tammy was riding a bucking bronco. Lana and Randy pulled the women apart, then stood between them.

Priscilla straightened out her jacket and flattened her skirt. "Greedy? We had two mills that were close in proximity and so badly mismanaged they were harming our profit margin. The merger made many employees redundant. Why do you think you are entitled to an extra bonus—one you didn't earn or deserve?"

"Even my boss agreed I was entitled to it."

"Several employees filed an appeal to the board of directors after that round of redundancies. That's why I denied all of them. I wasn't giving handouts or making exceptions. If you didn't work your full thirty years, you don't deserve a bonus."

"How can you be so cruel? I gave you twenty-nine years and seven months of my life and got the boot as thanks."

"Exactly—twenty-nine years, not thirty. And no one begged you to stay."

"I bet I worked for McGruffin longer than you did. With my seniority, I could have used that bonus to buy a condo in Florida I had my eye on and helped Hadley bankroll her business. You denied us our bonuses, yet, as I recall, you received a massive one after you retired."

"I contributed something unique to the company. Which is more than I can say for you, if you were one of those selected for redundancy."

"How dare you!" Tammy lunged at Priscilla. Her daughter and Randy held her back.

In the confusion, Anne was able to push her way through to Priscilla, jabbing the former CEO's chest with her forefinger. "Your tightfisted policies destroyed my business and left fifty of my employees without a job. And for what? To save a few bucks a year? McGruffin made record profits the next quarter."

"Who are you?" Priscilla asked, examining Anne with a frown.

"My company cleaned your corporate headquarters for ten years!"

Priscilla puffed up with pride. "Oh yes, you're that crazy bio-cleaner who sent all those threatening letters, aren't you? We were only able to make record profits the next quarter because of my required cutbacks and other cost-saving measures. There was so much excess fat that needed to be trimmed and too many external vendors—such as yourself—that were plucking us dry. Your profit margins are way too high. Your competition is fulfilling the same contract at almost half the cost."

"Because he employs illegal immigrants and uses off-shore tax shelters to avoid paying most of his taxes," Anne countered.

"It sounds like you could learn from him," Priscilla responded.

"You are as unethical as they come."

"I worked for McGruffin Wood's board of directors and company share-holders. They fully supported me and my policies."

"A healthy profit is all that matters to types like you, isn't it?" Anne interjected, not yet ready to let sleeping dogs lie.

Lana glanced over at Sara, Anne's mother, expecting her to be red with shame. Instead, she shone with pride as she watched her daughter stand up for herself. Lana couldn't help but smile despite the severity of the conversation.

Paige also appeared to be enjoying herself as the two women fought, Lana noticed, a smile forming on her lips as she wrote in her notebook.

Lana's initial knee-jerk reaction was to join in the lynching. McGruffin Wood had, after all, destroyed her career and life as she knew it. Only rationality caused her to stop and remember that Andersen hadn't been the CEO at the time of her libel lawsuit. Otherwise, she may have tried to murder her guest.

It took Lana quite a while to place E.P. Andersen's name. She was not one of the key players in Lana's investigation, so she hadn't spent much time looking into Priscilla's past. As far as Lana could recall, Priscilla was one of several vice presidents at McGruffin Wood at the time, but not one of those who knew about the company's polluting practices.

"What about the human cost? How many were laid off thanks to your cost-saving measures?" Tammy asked.

Priscilla looked at her in astonishment. "In your case, that merger saved McGruffin millions. It's never personal. It's all about the bottom line. If the company can't weather a storm, everybody loses," Priscilla explained, clearly satisfied with her response.

Daphne shook her head in disappointment. "You really are heartless, you know that?"

Before Lana or Randy could calm their guests, a receptionist entered the breakfast room and speed walked over to her. "Excuse me, but your taxi is here." The woman had to yell over the arguing guests to be heard.

Lana cursed silently under her breath. She was so distracted by the fighting, she had forgotten to check for the bus. "Thank you. We will be right there."

THE TOUR MUST GO ON

"Is everything alright here?" the receptionist asked.

"Yes, the group dynamic is off-kilter today, but nobody is going to kill anyone," Lana reassured the woman. "I apologize for disturbing your other guests," she added when she noticed several other of the hotel's patrons were watching her group closely.

"Ladies! Please calm down," Lana called out, then cleared her throat loudly several times until her group settled down.

Once they all turned towards her, she said, "Our taxi is here. This is supposed to be your vacation. I want to keep the rest of the day as confrontation-free as possible. Priscilla, for the sake of the group, I don't think you should join us," Lana said, albeit hesitantly. Priscilla was a paying guest, after all, and technically she had every right to join the tour. How she wished Dotty was here to help her decide what to do. She considered calling and asking for her advice, but the last thing she wanted to do was make Dotty feel as if she had to come downstairs and deal with this situation. She needed her rest in order to recover more quickly.

Priscilla tsked Lana's comment away. "Why not? This is my vacation with my daughter. We've paid for the right to be here."

Tammy cackled. "Really? You seem to be more interested in telling Paige about yourself than spending time with Daphne."

Lana ignored Tammy's barb, turning to her and Anne. "What about you two? Would you rather skip the tour, if Priscilla joins us?"

"I saved for years to be able to afford this trip. I am not letting her ruin this for me and Hadley," Tammy insisted. Her daughter locked arms with her mother in solidarity.

"Same here." Anne nodded in agreement, hugging her mother, Sara, tight.

Lana turned to Randy, her eyebrows raised. He shrugged in resignation.

"Okay, folks, the tour must go on," she said. "I guess we are all in this together."

16

The Windmills of Zaanse Schans

Before they boarded the bus for their short ride to Zaanse Schans, Lana and Randy took the precaution of splitting the group into two. Randy chose to lead Frieda, Franny, Anne, Sara, Tammy, and Hadley. The rest—Gillian, Priscilla, Daphne, and Paige—were Lana's responsibility. In hindsight, Lana was glad Dotty wasn't able to join them today. The older lady hated confrontations of any kind and would have felt somehow responsible for the bad vibes if she had been on the tour today.

On the ride over, Lana and Randy spent a few minutes consulting the map to see how their guests could experience all Zaanse Schans had to offer, without running into each other. Both quickly realized it was such a small town that it was going to be a challenge.

After a brief ride along the dikes protecting Amsterdam North from the River IJ, their bus turned inland and drove through a tapestry of pastures and water lands. They passed several small towns, but Lana didn't see any historic windmills, only modern ones. Lana noticed many homes had Dutch flags hanging at half-mast. She almost asked their driver what it signified until she recalled this was Remembrance Day in the Netherlands and much of Europe. Tomorrow was Liberation Day, marking the end of World War II. As much as she would have enjoyed taking part in the celebrations, Dotty had warned her that the city center was quite chaotic.

When their driver pulled into an enormous parking lot and turned off the engine, Randy and Lana looked around in confusion. When Lana had read about Zaanse Schans in her guidebooks, she had gotten the impression that it was a historical village that happened to have a few windmills. She hadn't realized it was a bona-fide tourist attraction that was sealed off with a fence.

Once they passed through the entrance gate, her group took in the tiny wooden houses, restaurants, souvenir shops, and canals. It matched exactly with the image of a traditional Dutch village she'd already formed in her mind. Signs to cheese shops, clog-making demonstrations, and the Albert Heijn Museum pointed to various paths leading through the small village. Rising in the distance was a dike built up along the River Zaan. A dozen traditional windmills were built on top of the steep embankment. Their shape reminded Lana of reed-covered salt shakers. The turning of their massive blades was a glorious sight.

Once their clients had taken the first round of photos, Randy went right, steering his group towards the Wooden Shoe Museum. Lana led her group through the village towards the River Zaan.

Her group took its time examining the small wooden houses, painted in deep greens and browns. Their pointed roofs and facades were decorated with colorful accents and an abundance of flower boxes. As they walked closer to one home and looked through the front windows, Lana was shocked to see how small it was. Most of the traditional homes they were walking past consisted of a small living room and kitchen downstairs, and a few tiny bedrooms upstairs. She couldn't imagine a modern family living comfortably in them.

After Lana and her group wound their way through the small village, they ascended a staircase leading up to the dike. A dirt path topped the embankment while a wider, concrete path ran parallel to its base. Lana's group chose the dirt path.

Lana took the lead. Priscilla and Paige walked side by side, so that, Lana assumed, the writer could continue interviewing the former CEO. Daphne seemed to be the only one interested in their surroundings and paused frequently to take pictures.

Gillian stuck to Lana like glue, but she didn't seem interested in conversing.

Strangely enough, her mother seemed more concerned with avoiding Priscilla than enjoying their visit to the village. *Did their business deal end so badly that Gillian was afraid Priscilla would suddenly recall the details and blow up?* Lana wondered. Something negative must have happened, she figured, otherwise her normally confident mother wouldn't have been acting like a child confronted with the presence of a forgetful bully. Lana watched Priscilla slyly, wondering when the former CEO would connect the dots and recognize her mother.

Priscilla, on the other hand, was so caught up in sharing her accomplishments with Paige that she didn't seem to notice anything else. Despite not wanting to have Paige join them today, Priscilla now seemed to be enjoying regaling the writer with colorful stories from her professional life. Her promise to Daphne of a real mother-daughter trip was apparently forgotten. From what Lana could overhear, Priscilla had certainly led an interesting life and was quite successful, but she was so extraordinarily self-centered it was hard to root for her. *I guess she would have to be, to have climbed so high up the corporate ladder so quickly*, she reckoned. Priscilla was not only one of the first women to lead McGruffin Wood, but she was also the youngest person to hold the position, from what Lana had gathered.

Despite Gillian's best attempts to use Lana as a shield, within such a small group, Priscilla was bound to notice her sooner or later. When they entered the fence surrounding De Kat, a windmill famous for making paint, the two women almost bumped into each other. Gillian ducked away, but Priscilla snapped her fingers.

"I figured out how we know each other. You run Hansen Advertising Agency, don't you?" the former CEO asked.

"Yes, that's right. We worked together once," Gillian responded and started to walk away in an obvious attempt at cutting off the conversation.

"You did the impossible and managed to turn public opinion back around, after that horrible lawsuit. We were all quite grateful," Priscilla called after her.

Gillian froze, then whipped around to face her. "My team did all the work—I had nothing to do with it."

To Lana, her mother didn't look proud, but distraught. *What the heck was going on?* she wondered.

"Nonsense. Without your leadership, drive, and vision, the agency wouldn't have such a strong reputation."

Priscilla then turned to Paige. "That reminds me of another story I should tell you about. It happened before I was appointed CEO, but it's partly why I was able to ascend so quickly," she said to Paige as they walked towards the entrance to the windmill.

Curious to hear the story, Lana started to follow, but Gillian grabbed her arm. "You do know that I don't lead all of the advertising campaigns my agency is responsible for, right?"

Lana looked at her, puzzled. "I didn't, but I guess I do now."

"Most of the time, I don't know who the clients are until the projects are well underway. We are too simply large for me to keep tabs on them all."

"Okay," Lana said, then paused a beat. "Why are you telling me this?"

"I, uh, it just came into my head," Gillian mumbled.

"If you aren't leading project teams anymore, what do you do these days?" Lana asked, keeping her tone gentle. Lana figured any attempt at making conversation—however clunky—was an olive branch that she should not push away. So far, all of their exchanges on this trip had ended up with one insulting or offending the other—intentionally or not. And their contact over the past decade had been so sporadic that neither really knew much about the other's personal or professional lives.

"It changes day by day. I usually sit in on the portfolio review sessions of our largest campaigns, but I spend most of my time meeting with potential clients around the country."

"That's great that you get to travel around the United States. Are you still happy?"

Gillian let out a sigh. "That is a great question. I was, until a few months ago. Now I'm thinking of taking a step back and letting my senior staff take on more of the workload."

"Is something wrong?" Lana asked, suddenly remembering that her mother had recently begun reaching out to her on social media. Though they didn't talk much anymore, Lana hoped that Gillian would have called her if she was sick.

"No, I'm not ill or anything like that." Gillian smiled, evidently touched by Lana's concern. "Barry and I are talking about buying a motor home so we can explore more of the country together. But as long as I continue working eighty-hour weeks, we won't be able to do that."

"What does Barry do for a living?" She knew he and Gillian had been dating for several years, but Lana had not yet met or spoken to him. It felt strange to think that her mother wanted to marry and spend her life with someone she had never even seen before.

"He founded several successful internet startups, but he sold the last one a few months ago. Since then, he's been planning a series of dream vacations for us to go on," Gillian said. Her face softened and her voice sparkled when she talked about her fiancé.

"That's wonderful. I do hope it all works out for you." Lana gave her mother a spontaneous hug. After a moment's hesitation, Gillian's stiff posture softened in her daughter's arms.

Over her mother's shoulder, Lana could see the Group of Three were waiting by the ticket counter, watching Lana and Gillian. A line was already forming behind them. "I would love to see a photo of Barry, but right now, we better catch up with the rest."

17

Terrorists and Bomb Scares

Lana worked her way through the crowd and paid for their tickets before allowing her guests to enter first. As she did, Lana noticed Randy's group entering the gate to De Kat. "Uh oh," she muttered, and rushed her group inside.

The first thing she noticed was the air. Lana choked on the bits of powder floating around the room like a thin mist. The space was fairly dark and only lit by a few small windows. Towards the back were enormous wooden cogs and beams turning a massive grindstone around in a circle. The stone, in turn, crushed white chunks of what looked like chalk into a fine powder. The wood and stone groaned and creaked loudly as the wheel sped up, then slowed down.

Lana was captivated. The inner workings of a windmill were far more complex than she had imagined, yet extremely compact and efficient in design.

Her group examined the displays explaining how the chunks of chalk-like substance were slowly reduced to a powder by being repeatedly pummeled and crushed by a series of stone discs, each as broad in diameter as Lana was tall.

A sign attracted her attention, warning guests that visiting the windmill was at their own risk. When Lana saw a mother swatting her child's hand away from the turning stone wheel and noticed that there was no rope holding visitors back, she understood the need for a legal disclaimer.

Out of the corner of her eye, she saw Randy in line for tickets. Since her group's attention seemed to be waning, Lana said, "Why don't we head upstairs?"

She hoped they could get up to the next level before Randy's group entered the same space. In the center of the windmill was a small hole cut out of the ceiling. Light from above shone through like rays of sunshine. A narrow, wooden ladder was the only way up.

Daphne went first, and Gillian headed up the rear. Lana waited until her mother had stepped onto the next floor before starting up. Lana grabbed hold and felt her grip slipping. The ladder were so old and had been used so often, the wood felt slippery.

These ladders would not be allowed in the United States, Lana thought. She sure hoped Randy could help get Frieda and Sara safely upstairs; one wrong step meant a fall of several feet onto a hard, stone floor. She kept her gaze skyward and climbed as quickly as she dared to the second-floor landing. When Lana's foot slid off one of the rungs, she grabbed on tight and hoped her older clients skipped the ladders altogether.

When they reached the second floor, Lana was amazed to see they were face to face with a mass of cogged wheels and turning beams, lightly sprinkled with white dust. This was the heart of the windmill, she realized, watching in fascination as the machinery slowed and sped up, depending on how fast the blades turned. A thick shaft of wood went straight up the center of the windmill to the third floor, where it attached to the turning blades. The entire floor shuddered a little, and the sound was almost deafening.

A narrow space provided enough room to walk around the mechanism. Out of the many windows, Lana could see the River Zaan and the vast pasturelands behind the village.

There were so many tourists, she and her group had to wait in line to climb up to the next level. When they reached the third and top floor, the room was even smaller than the last one, though there was more space for visitors to move around in. Here the wheels connecting the turning blades and rotating shaft were visible. The large wooden beam spun quickly, powering the cogged wheels and grindstone below.

The windows on this floor looked out onto a wide platform skirting the windmill's body. Lana couldn't wait to check out the views. She looked around to locate her group amongst the many tourists squeezed into the space. Paige, Daphne, Priscilla, and Gillian were all in line to ascend the staircase leading out onto the balcony. Lana joined them.

The views from the balcony were lovely. From here, she could see far down the river, most of the neighboring city of Zaandam, and all of the windmills on the dike.

Lana followed the railing around the platform, her progress slowed by the many visitors snapping photographs. The balcony was much wider than she expected, which was handy considering how many tourists were out on it. As she walked around the structure, she could hear the blades whooshing by before she could see them.

When she reached the blades, a rickety fence made out of a few pieces of wood blocked visitors' access. Lana didn't need to read the sign to understand why. The windmill's four blades turned so quickly that Lana imagined one blow to the head would be fatal.

Gillian was standing by the railing, watching barges and boats sailing the River Zaan. She was easy to spot in her new color-block skirt and bright blue blouse. When Lana joined her, Gillian smiled as she took her hand. A week ago, Lana couldn't imagine standing contentedly next to her mother. *Dotty was right*, she realized; without coming on this trip together, neither one would have made time for the other. They had hurt each other so often with their barbs and button-pushing that neither one was willing to give the other a break.

Lana was relaxing into her mother's company when Tammy's voice drew her attention. Randy's group had arrived. Lana hoped there wouldn't be any more squabbles today. She could hear Tammy complaining to Randy about the steepness of the stairs as they walked closer.

All of a sudden, Tammy raced to the railing, close to where Lana was standing, and waved.

"Hello, Hadley! I made it!" she yelled down to her daughter.

Lana looked down at the lawn where Hadley stood, waving back at her mother and taking photos of her in goofy poses.

A few feet behind Hadley stood Frieda and Sara. They and everyone else on the grass below appeared to be doll-sized, and Lana realized that she and her group were much higher up than she'd thought. When her guests noticed Lana up on the balcony, they also began waving.

Lana was returning Frieda and Sara's waves when a yell from Hadley caused her hand to freeze.

"Could you stop that? You're ruining Mom's photos," she admonished.

Lana looked around in confusion before realizing that Tammy was standing so close to her that Lana was unwittingly in the background of Hadley's photos. Lana scooted farther down the railing, so as to not accidentally photobomb the older woman.

As soon as Tammy and Randy moved on, Daphne and Priscilla came up to the railing and stood close to Lana, their gazes also focused on the gray-blue water and wooden houses lining the opposite riverbank.

Gillian bristled slightly when Priscilla approached, but did her best to ignore the recent retiree. Anne and Franny came around the bend and spotted the others. When Anne saw Priscilla was among them, she pulled a face and changed direction, taking Franny with her.

"It's like stepping back in time, isn't it?" Daphne said to her mother.

"It is so quaint," Priscilla agreed. "I haven't thanked you yet for booking this trip, Daphne. It's good to get away. Adjusting to retirement has been far more difficult than I imagined. I am so used to having a busy schedule and a line of people wanting to know my opinion. It's hard to get used to the fact that they no longer care."

"Is that why you invited Paige along?"

Priscilla squeezed her daughter's shoulder. "I'm afraid so. But don't worry, I already talked with Dotty, and she won't be a problem much longer."

"What do you mean?" Daphne asked as Paige approached them.

Paige's walk slowed to a crawl, and her eyes narrowed. Lana wondered how much of Priscilla and Daphne's conversation the writer had heard.

Paige had looked like she wanted to speak to Priscilla, but instead, she turned to Gillian and asked brightly, "So Gillian, Priscilla just told me about how your agency helped McGruffin Wood recover from a libel lawsuit against the *Seattle Chronicle* ten years ago. Your team was able to turn that negative publicity around, despite the accusations of environmental pollution. I would love to interview you about it, as filler for the book."

Lana shook her head, certain her ears were playing tricks on her. "What did you just say?"

"That your mother helped McGruffin Wood recover from the bad publicity your libel lawsuit caused."

As Paige's words sank in, Lana gripped the railing so tightly her knuckles felt as if they were about to burst through her skin. She and Gillian hadn't always gotten along, but she couldn't believe that her own mother would be heartless enough to help the company that ruined her life.

"No, that can't be…" Her words trailed off. Lana turned to Gillian, but her mother refused to meet her eye.

"Can I interview you, too?" Paige asked Lana, seemingly oblivious to how painful her accusations were. "I'm curious to hear how you feel about the Hansen Advertising Agency's role in the recovery of McGruffin, the same company that ultimately destroyed your career."

Lana's body started to tremble, her mind unwilling to process the writer's words. "Tell me it's not true," she whimpered.

Gillian turned to Lana and held her hands tight. "I didn't know about the campaign until it was too late to cancel it."

Lana felt as if someone had sucker punched her. "How could you help McGruffin, after all they did to me?"

Priscilla stared at Gillian. "Wow, that's pretty heartless."

"You're one to talk," Paige goaded. "It was your idea to pay off the whistleblower so he wouldn't testify about your company's environmental pollution. That seems even more heartless, if you ask me."

"What do you mean, Priscilla paid off the whistleblower?" Lana thought back to her main source. A senior analyst, he had come to her with reports proving McGruffin Wood was intentionally dumping more chemicals than was allowed into local waterways, which had caused a massive salmon starvation. Up until a week before the court date, her source had been gung-ho about bringing McGruffin Wood down.

Which had made his sudden reluctance to testify in court even more painful. When he called her mere days before their court date and explained that he was backing out, Lana figured it was nerves and had begged him to testify regardless. He cited his need to protect his family against the anonymous threats sent to his home. After showing her the letters, he refused to meet with or speak to Lana again. Her source's refusal to testify meant the documents he had provided were trivialized by McGruffin Wood's lawyers—and that the corporation easily won the libel lawsuit.

"The whistleblower and his family feared for their lives," she said numbly. Lana's mind was reeling. Her whole world and everything she had believed for the past ten years was being turned on its head.

"No, that's what Priscilla told him to say. It was her idea to hire a private investigator to find and pay off your source. That's why she was tapped as CEO after the scandal blew over. McGruffin offered your whistleblower a half-million dollars to keep his mouth shut. He pushed for double that amount. Since cleanup would have cost several times more, they took the deal. McGruffin Wood made out like bandits."

Lana's brain put the facts into a row. "He destroyed my life for money?" Her source had lied about the threats to his family to get Lana off his back. The company had gotten away with environmental pollution. And her mother had helped it recover from its public relations nightmare. Lana felt fractured and confused. She leaned heavily against the railing, trying to take in what this meant.

"Is that true? Did you really pay him off?" Daphne asked. When Priscilla refused to make eye contact, Daphne looked at her mother with such disgust. "You are a monster!" she said before storming away.

As Paige's words continued to sink in, all Lana could see was red. She turned to Priscilla.

"Are you that *Seattle Chronicle* reporter?" Priscilla asked, a bemused expression on her face. "I never expected to meet you. You cost us a pretty penny, but that lawsuit was my shortcut to the top."

She chuckled as she examined Lana from top to toe. "And your mother brought our company back into the public's good graces. How rich."

Priscilla's tone was so jovial, something in Lana snapped. An overwhelming desire to shut the recent retiree up consumed her. A primal scream erupted out of her. Her hands wrapped around Priscilla's throat as she pushed the older woman backwards. They crashed against the thin fence cordoning off the turning blades. Priscilla scratched at Lana's hands with her manicured fingernails, desperate to breathe.

As the blood boiled in Lana's veins, it was as if someone turned on the mute button. Others screamed and pulled on her arms, but all Lana was aware of was Priscilla's reddening face—and of the deep joy that seeing her die would bring.

"You destroyed my life for money!" Lana screeched, shaking Priscilla so violently that they broke through the thin fence. Lana was vaguely aware of the snapped wood and screams erupting all around. She kept pushing Priscilla backwards until she could feel the strong wind, stirred up by broad wooden blades whooshing by.

Lana took note of the blades' position and changed direction, aiming Priscilla's body towards them.

"Stop—she's not worth it!" Gillian tugged on her daughter's arms and hands. "She's already taken so much from you. Don't let her take your freedom, as well."

Lana looked into Priscilla's bulging eyes and saw real fear. She released her hands, mortified that she had let her emotions get so out of control. Priscilla fell to the floor and began gasping air back into her lungs.

Gillian pulling on her arm broke Lana's trance. As if someone turned the sound back on, Lana was suddenly aware of other tourists screaming for security and running every which way. Splintered wood from the thin railing was spread across the windmill's balcony. Blood ran from a long gash on her right arm. Lana had no idea how she'd cut herself, until she saw part of the railing was covered in red.

Feeling ashamed and betrayed, Lana shook off Gillian's hand and ran through the mass of tourists congregating around the staircase, all trying to get down as quickly as possible. Screams of "terrorists," "murder," and "bomb" echoed through the windmill's core.

Lana pushed an older couple aside and practically slid down the ladder to the second floor. There, even more tourists were crushed around the ladder, pushing and shoving each other as they all tried to get downstairs. Screams of panic and fear wafted up all around her.

The jam of bodies blocking the ladders was too thick to push through. Unable to get out, Lana collapsed onto the floor, crying. Soon two security guards burst through the throng, pushing their way up the ladders.

"Are you hurt, ma'am?" one asked Lana as his colleague continued up to the top floor.

Lana looked up at him through bleary eyes. "I'm okay," she stammered.

He held out a hand to help her up. She began to stand when a flash of color passing in front of the window drew their attention.

"What was that?" the guard muttered as he helped Lana rise.

Moments later, they got their answer. Blood-curdling screams arose from the lawn. Lana pushed her face to the window's pane. Far below was Priscilla, spread out on the grass, her arms and legs extended like a snow angel. Blood pouring from her skull was slowly forming a halo around her head.

18

The Truth Will Come Out

"It's all clear," the leader of the bomb squad announced to the lead investigator. Lana and her group were standing on the concrete path running along the dike, far from De Kat windmill. Clusters of tourists were spread out along the path, all answering police officers' questions about what they had seen and had been doing when Priscilla plummeted to her death.

The many screams about terrorists and bombs meant a special team had to search through the windmill for any explosive devices before the police and forensics team could enter.

A convoy of ambulances were taking the stream of visitors with broken hips, arms, and legs away. Lana felt guilty as she watched the many tourists being moved into the awaiting vehicles. They had misinterpreted her fight with Priscilla and outburst afterwards as a terror attack, causing a mass panic and many broken bones as a result.

Because Priscilla was in her group, the lead investigator was interviewing them. They were more somber than normal as they dealt with the unexpected death of a fellow guest in differing ways. Even though most didn't know or like Priscilla, it was clearly still traumatic for all of them.

Hadley was visibly shaking. Priscilla's body had landed a mere foot from where she was standing, and she was having trouble controlling her emotions. Tammy stroked her hair and wiped away her daughter's tears.

Frieda and Sara held their daughters tight. Only Paige, Daphne, and Gillian stood well apart from the rest. Lana was raw with emotion but was doing her best to remain professional. She was incredibly grateful that Dotty had made Randy the lead guide. He was stoic and rational as he handed copies of their client list to the investigator and answered his questions about their itinerary and movements.

"It appears your guest, Erin Priscilla Andersen, was hit by one of the windmill's blades and knocked off the balcony. I understand you, Lana Hansen, and the victim were responsible for breaking the fence cordoning off the blades. That's extremely dangerous. Can you explain how the fence was broken?"

"We were standing next to the railing on the observation deck close to the fence when we began to argue. In the heat of the moment, I pushed her." Lana's voice faltered. "And we broke the fence in our fall."

"It must have been some fight to warrant that strong of a reaction."

"Yes, it was."

"Why were you fighting?"

"Priscilla destroyed my life," Lana whispered.

The inspector's forehead furrowed. "Can you be more specific?"

Lana bit her lip, trying to figure out how to best describe how exactly Priscilla had harmed her, when Paige announced quite loudly, "Priscilla was responsible for ruining Lana's career in journalism."

Lana looked at Paige, startled.

"How did she manage to do this?" the inspector asked Paige, but kept his eyes on Lana.

"Lana had been investigating Priscilla's company, McGruffin Wood, and they sued her for libel. Priscilla paid off Lana's source so he wouldn't testify, and thanks to her, McGruffin won the lawsuit and Lana lost her job at the *Seattle Chronicle*," Paige explained, as if she was being helpful.

What is the writer playing at? Lana wondered.

"Is this true?" the officer asked Lana.

"Yes, but I didn't know that Priscilla had paid off my source until this afternoon. It was quite upsetting."

"Hmm, interesting," the inspector mumbled as he made notes on a small pad in his hand.

"And where were you when Priscilla fell?" he asked Lana.

"On the second floor. A security guard and I were standing close to a window and saw her fall." Lana shivered uncontrollably as the image of Priscilla's body racing by flashed through her mind.

The inspector snapped his fingers. "That's right, the guard already gave us his statement. I did not know you were the guest he was assisting."

When the inspector turned to Paige, Lana felt as if a weight had been lifted from her shoulders.

"And where were you when Priscilla fell?" he asked the writer.

"I was waiting to descend the ladder to the second floor, when I heard screams coming from outside. I went back out onto the balcony to see what was going on, and then I saw Priscilla's body on the ground."

Tammy looked up at Paige. "Funny, I was standing by the ladder and don't recall seeing you come inside. Weren't you still out on the platform when she fell?"

"If I were the police, you would be my prime suspect," Paige countered, ignoring Tammy's question. "After all, you were the one who said you would kill Priscilla if you ever met her."

"How could I know she was on our trip?" Tammy glanced at the policeman nervously. "Besides, I said that in the heat of the moment."

"Wait, you also knew the victim?" the inspector asked Tammy.

"Yes, I worked at one of McGruffin Wood's paper mills."

"And yet you did not recognize her?" It was obvious from his tone that the officer did not believe Tammy.

"McGruffin Wood employs more than a half-million people in Washington state alone. I worked at one of their subsidiaries, but I had never met her. Why would I know what she looks like? She was a name on the letterhead and my paychecks, that's all."

The officer's eyes narrowed as he wrote down her statement.

"If you're looking for suspects, Priscilla ruined Anne's cleaning company. She's got more of a reason to kill Priscilla than I do," Tammy added.

"You have got to be joking," Sara piped up, in Anne's defense. "My daughter may have lost the McGruffin Wood contract, but she has a roof over her head and food in her belly. Once she's got a few new clients, she'll be back on her feet. She's got no reason to harm anyone."

"Is this true? Did Priscilla ruin your company?" The policeman ignored Sara and focused his attention on Anne instead.

"Not directly. One of her policy changes meant I lost the contract to clean their offices. But we aren't bankrupt yet," Anne said, her chin jutted out. To Lana, she sounded more confident now than she had since this trip began.

"If your company is experiencing financial difficulties, why are you on vacation?"

"Because I paid for it, long before her company got into trouble," Sara said, again answering before her daughter could. Anne seemed happy enough to let her mother do the talking.

The officer nodded and filled his notebook with her words.

Daphne examined Anne through squinted eyes. "But you did send my mom threatening letters, didn't you?"

"Says you," Anne retorted.

"For the past ten years, I have been her personal assistant, and I have access to all of her correspondence. She asked me to keep a file of all the threats she received when she was CEO. I'm certain yours are in there."

"How dare you implicate me in Priscilla's murder!" Anne screeched.

The policeman stepped in between the two women. "Let me reiterate, we have no reason to suspect foul play at this point. I am merely trying to discern who was where when Miss Andersen fell." He looked to Anne, questioningly.

"I didn't hurt her! I was on the ladder going down to the second floor when I heard the screams," Anne explained.

"And I was on the lawn with Frieda," Sara said as her friend nodded in agreement.

"My knees aren't made for climbing ladders anymore," Frieda added.

"And where were you, miss?" The officer looked to Franny.

"Anne and I were coming downstairs. I had just reached the first floor and Anne was a few rungs above me, when I heard the screams."

The inspector made a few notes, then turned his attention to Gillian.

"Where were you when Priscilla fell?"

Gillian looked at the officer and blinked. "What?"

Lana had never seen her mother so pale. Her eyes were unfocused, and her body was trembling. She wondered whether Gillian had been following the conversation.

The officer repeated his question as concern and suspicion crossed his face.

"I, ah, was trying to follow Lana downstairs, but security guards were coming up the ladder so I had to wait. When the first guard reached the top floor, I heard the screams coming from below."

"Can anyone verify your statement? Did you see anyone else from your group?"

Gillian's forehead creased in confusion. "I don't know. I just wanted to catch up to Lana. I wasn't paying attention to anyone else."

The investigator turned once again to Lana. "Did you see your mother coming after you?"

Lana locked eyes with Gillian. "No, I did not. The last time I saw her, my mother was still outside on the platform with Priscilla. I didn't see her running after me."

Gillian looked so hurt and confused, but Lana couldn't have cared less. After what Gillian had done to help McGruffin Wood, she deserved it.

The officer silently wrote down her statement, then closed his notebook and stood before them.

"Thank you for your statements. At this time, I will ask Daphne to accompany us and her mother to the hospital. We do ask that you make yourselves available, in case we have more questions or need further clarification."

Lana took out her business card. "If you do have more questions for any of us, you can call me anytime. We are in the Netherlands for six more days."

"Thank you." The officer pocketed the card and waited for Daphne to join him on his walk to his car.

"I want to come, too," Paige piped up as she stepped in line behind Daphne.

The blonde woman turned around and hissed, "You are not family and certainly not welcome to join us. I don't need you pecking at my mother's bones."

Paige stood stock still as Daphne and the officers walked away. The twisted grimace on the writer's face sent chills down Lana's spine.

19

Lessons in Forgiveness

When Gillian knocked on her hotel room door, Lana was still reeling from the shocking news of Priscilla's bribery and her mother's betrayal. The last thing she wanted to do was to talk to Gillian. However, she was even more unwilling to make their argument public. Lana stepped back and let her mother inside.

When Gillian tried to touch her, Lana pulled away and crossed her arms tightly over her chest. "How could you?"

Gillian stood before her, her head hanging low.

"After what McGruffin did to me, my career, my life, you took them on as a client? Aren't you rich enough? Did you really need to take their money, too?"

Gillian shook her head vehemently. "It's not like that. The agency has grown exponentially since your father died. Ten years ago, we were in an expansion phase, and I was crisscrossing the country to help get our new branches up and running. After I got back to Seattle, I sat in on a few review sessions, and one happened to be for McGruffin Wood. It was a shock to discover that they were one of our new clients."

Lana cackled. "A shock, huh? But not enough of one to cancel the project?"

"In hindsight, I should have. But my team had already invested hundreds of hours into the ad campaign by the time I saw –"

Lana held up her hand. "Stop. I don't want to hear your excuses. I am your daughter, and McGruffin Wood ruined my life. I cannot believe you would be associated with them in any way."

"Lana, I never meant to –"

Lana crossed to her door and pulled it open. "I don't want to hear it. Get out."

"I am on your tour. You are going to have to deal with me at some point."

"Maybe. But not right now. And don't you dare show up for our day trip tomorrow. I will not allow you to mess up this job for me."

Gillian walked over to Lana and gently pushed the door shut. "I can't make up for the past ten years. And as painful as it was for you to find out this way, at least you now know the truth. Ever since I found out about my agency's involvement with McGruffin, I haven't been able to face you. I feel horrible that we helped the company that destroyed your career recover from the libel lawsuit."

"Is that why you stopped taking my calls?"

Gillian hung her head in shame. "Yes," she whispered. "Keeping you at a distance wasn't the best approach, I admit that. But our relationship was already so tattered. Whenever we did see each other, I lashed out, in frustration. My agency didn't do anything wrong by taking McGruffin on as a client, but I know you wouldn't see it that way."

"You're right. I don't see it that way." Lana ripped the door open. "Get out."

Gillian shook her head as she exited. As soon as her mother was out of sight, Lana raced down the hallway to Dotty's room, tears already forming in her eyes.

20

Don't Give Up

Lana blew her nose loudly into a fifth Kleenex as tears streamed down her cheeks.

Dotty sat next to her on the hotel room bed, stroking Lana's dark-brown hair. "My tummy's finally settled down. I can take over as guide, if you need time off or want to go home."

Lana knew Dotty was more than capable of filling her shoes, but she had been so sick that she had been confined to her hotel room all day. As much as Lana was hurting inside, she couldn't ask her boss to step in. What Dotty needed most was to relax and unwind so she could heal properly—not to get stressed out by working.

Dotty's sincerity and willingness to help dried Lana's tears. She took the older lady's hands and squeezed them gently. "I certainly appreciate you offering, but no thank you. I can do this. I refuse to let Gillian ruin my job, as well."

Dotty sucked in her breath. "Gillian didn't have anything to do with you getting fired. You have to forgive her, Lana. She is your mother. And I do believe her when she says that she didn't know McGruffin was a client, at least not at first."

"But when she did find out, she didn't cancel the project," Lana said, feeling helpless.

Dotty shrugged. "Business is business, Lana. It sounds like her team had already put in a whole lot of work on McGruffin's advertising campaign before she even knew about it. And if she had pulled the plug, it would have been difficult to explain to her crew and client why she did. It may also have created image problems for her within her agency or even caused other clients to look elsewhere. She has a company full of workers to consider."

"But –"

"Lana, making difficult decisions is all part of being the boss. You should never take it personally. To be honest, if I was in your mother's shoes, I probably would have done the same."

Lana's jaw dropped in shock.

Dotty shrugged.

Lana closed her eyes, taking in her boss's rational explanation. As painful as it was to accept, Dotty did have a point. Lana opened her eyes slowly. "I guess if I hadn't gotten fired, I never would have met you. So something good came out of all this."

Dotty hugged her tight. "I sure am sorry that I invited Gillian along without asking you first. I should have asked more about your past before I pushed my nose in. But I truly thought it would be a good way for you two to get through this impasse. I mean, neither one of you was picking up the phone to make lunch dates."

"You are right about that. We were getting along better than we have in years," Lana admitted. "At least, until Paige told me about McGruffin being a client of Mom's ad agency."

Lana's mind flashed back to the windmill. "The real villain here is Priscilla. I cannot believe she bribed the whistleblower. Do you know my source showed me a pile of threatening notes his family received? It was because of those letters that I could not, in good conscience, push him to testify. And they were all fakes!"

Lana rose and began pacing the room. "If that libel suit had never happened, I would still be doing what I loved most. And I was so good at it, too. But greed took it away from me. I'm glad Priscilla is dead."

"Hush, child! No one deserves to die," Dotty chided. "You're good at being a tour guide and lots of other things. You may not win any more awards, but you make people feel good about themselves."

Lana heard Dotty's words, but as the repercussions of Priscilla's actions sunk in, she felt as if her universe was collapsing. Her career in journalism—her passion in life—had been taken away from her for no good reason. She had always known she was innocent, but having the world tell her she was not had put a major dent in her self-esteem. For years, she hadn't dared to write a word, for fear that her old colleagues would find out about it. All of those years wasted, simply because her source had chosen a million dollars over his conscience. It was almost too much to bear.

"It's not fair," Lana cried out.

"Honey, life isn't always fair, and no amount of money can guarantee that everything will work out the way you want it to. It's how you roll with the punches that life throws you, Lana, that matters most. And from where I'm standing, you're doing pretty well."

Lana stopped pacing and looked to Dotty.

"You have your health, caring colleagues, a cat who adores you, a good group of friends, and your boss is pretty nice, too," Dotty said with a smile. "Don't give up, Lana. You're stronger than this. And a whole lot of people have got your back."

Lana looked glumly at the floor.

"If the truth comes out about this whistleblower, would you want to go back to journalism?"

Lana froze. Dotty had a point. If the whistleblower did come clean about taking a bribe, she would finally be able to prove to the world that she had not made up her sources all those years ago.

"I honestly never considered it," Lana said. "Yes" was on the tip of her tongue, but something made her hesitate.

"Oh no, I have to call Jeremy! He lost his job, too, as a result of the libel lawsuit. He'll want to know about this straightaway. But I bet he won't believe me."

21

Journalist Vindicated?

"I cannot believe it. You mean to tell me your source took a million-dollar bribe to not testify? He showed us all those letters threatening his family. I can't believe we fell for it," Jeremy moaned into the phone, his anger coursing through the international line.

"Not only did we lose our jobs, it took the *Seattle Chronicle* years to recover financially," he continued. "I had to take a huge step backwards, career-wise, to survive. And I know how hard you've had it, after all those horrible stories about you intentionally falsifying your research were published. It is unbelievable what greed can do to a person's moral compass."

"I agree –" Lana began, but Jeremy was too worked up to listen and talked right over her.

"I am going to get my best reporters working on this right away. We shouldn't have much trouble finding your source. And when we do, he and McGruffin Wood are going to be the front-page story for weeks. I bet the *Seattle Chronicle* will want to file a lawsuit to get their money back and set the record straight."

Lana thought of her old colleagues at the *Seattle Chronicle*. Within days of her firing, most had turned on her, publicly stating in newspapers and on television that she was a shame to the profession. How would they react when they found out that Lana had not been lying? Would they welcome her back with open arms? Would job offers roll in? Or would the stain of the libel lawsuit tarnish any chance of returning to her old vocation?

More importantly, could she forgive and forget?

Investigative journalism had been her joy and calling in life. But after ten years of being shunned by her old colleagues and unable to practice her dream profession, she didn't know what she would do when this news hit the papers. The joy she had initially felt at finally seeing her name cleared was tempered by the fact that she would now be the main story—"Journalist Vindicated After Ten Years" would make a wonderful headline.

"Priscilla's daughter was also her personal assistant, and she is on my tour," Lana said. "They didn't get along that well. I'll ask if she has any documents proving her mother paid off my source, if he doesn't come clean straight away."

"A million dollars is hard to hide. If we can find the money, it will be pretty difficult for him to cover it up."

Lana nodded, even though Jeremy couldn't see her. "That's an excellent point. I have another scoop for you that you might want to include in your coverage."

"There's more?"

"Yes. My mother's advertising agency was responsible for McGruffin's advertising after the trial."

"Ouch. Did she work directly on the McGruffin ads?"

"I'm not entirely certain."

"Look, Lana, I know you and your mother don't see eye to eye, but before I have my team investigate that aspect, why don't you do some digging around."

When she remained silent, Jeremy added, "It would be far less embarrassing for Gillian than having my team get in touch with her employees. She is, after all, your mother."

"You're right. Mom said she was out of town when McGruffin Wood contacted her agency. I'll give her assistant a call and see if she has access to Mom's old agendas. That should clear this up."

"That sounds like a good idea. I'm going to keep your mom's involvement private for now. Why don't you keep me updated?"

"I will. And please call or email me the second you find my old source. I cannot wait to hear his side of the story. Let that weasel try to lie his way out of this one."

22

Keukenhof Gardens

May 5—Day Four of the Wanderlust Tour in Keukenhof Gardens

"Welcome to the Keukenhof, the largest flower garden in Europe!" Lana exclaimed, as her group passed through the entrance gates. She didn't have to fake her enthusiasm. Even through the mass of tourists milling around, she could tell it was gorgeous. Based on her guests' expressions, they were as excited to be here as she was.

She walked them over to a river of blue flowers flowing through a field of orange tulips, so that Randy could locate their guide. Lana breathed in the perfume of hundreds of petals and pollen, reveling in the sweet and earthy fragrances.

It felt strange to be back in front of the group and pretending as if nothing out of the ordinary had happened yesterday. Lana had expected her guests would be somber and quiet today. But they were quite the opposite. If anything, the mood was upbeat and jovial.

Tammy had already gotten in touch with her old boss and asked whether it was possible to appeal Priscilla's decision and claim her bonus after all. Apparently he had always been sweet on her and was quite pleased to hear from her again. On the bus ride over, she couldn't stop talking about how accommodating he was being to her request.

Even Anne had a new spring to her step. Her hair was freshly washed, and her clothes appeared to be clean for a change. It was almost as if Priscilla's death had lifted a weight that had been holding the business owner down.

Yet what shocked Lana most of all was how chipper and perky Daphne was. One would never have guessed that the woman had lost her mother the previous afternoon. Was this front of positivity and normality her way of dealing with the grief? Or was she truly happy that her mother was gone? Even now she had a smile on her face as she messaged her boyfriend. Since Priscilla's death, her daughter hadn't let her telephone go. As strange as her reaction seemed, Lana tried not to judge Daphne, knowing that everyone dealt with death in different ways.

Lana only wished she could forget about her own mother's betrayal so easily. Every time she thought of Gillian, her heart turned to stone. Despite Dotty's assurances that it was just business, Lana could not accept that her mother had been so callous. McGruffin Wood had destroyed her life, and Gillian's agency had resurrected its reputation afterwards. She tried reminding herself that Dotty admitted she would have done the same, but the pain was too fresh.

Thankfully Gillian hadn't come down to the lobby this morning. When Randy went up to her room, she made clear to him that she would steer clear of Lana until her daughter wanted her to be around. Lana smirked; that wasn't going to happen anytime soon.

Gillian's betrayal stung so badly that Lana had trouble keeping her eyes dry. She made a mental note to get in touch with Gillian's assistant after today's tour. If her mother had indeed been out of town when her agency signed McGruffin Wood as a client, then it would help soften the blow.

As much as she wanted to be investigating Priscilla's story about the whistleblower, Lana knew there was nothing she could do right now but wait. Knowing Jeremy was on the case was the only thing keeping her sane. And today's tour would help keep her mind off of the case, she reckoned.

Try as she might, she couldn't stop thinking about Jeremy and the whistleblower on the ride over. Would Jeremy find the man? Or had he taken the money and made a new life for himself somewhere far from Seattle? Lana would give anything to be the one to interview him. What excuse would her source use to justify his abhorrent behavior? Did he know he had destroyed Lana's and Jeremy's careers? And did he even care?

Lana was glad that Jeremy still worked in journalism, though not at the *Seattle Chronicle*, and could assign his reporters to the story instead of turning to their former colleagues. Based on how quick her coworkers at the *Chronicle* had been to cast Lana out, she doubted they would be able to remain objective.

Randy waved, and Lana navigated her group through the thick crowds to the awaiting guide. Dotty and Sally, walking arm in arm, brought up the rear. Dotty refused to miss another day of the tour, but she was still off-balance and looked so vulnerable. Lana was glad she hadn't asked her to step in as a guide today.

A tall, blond man welcomed them to the park and immediately launched into his practiced speech.

"It a pleasure to welcome you to the Keukenhof. It is an exhibition garden showcasing flowers grown by some of the finest bulb producers in the Netherlands. Sixteen hundred varieties of flowers are planted each year in our eighty acres of gardens. I will lead you along the main paths and explain more about the varieties you see. Shall we begin?"

Lana drifted towards the back of her group, glad the guide would be keeping them entertained for the next hour. As much as she wanted to crawl back into bed and pretend yesterday never happened, it was probably better to be out among the bursts of color and happy people.

She watched as Daphne pulled out her phone and began typing in a message. When Daphne's phone pinged seconds later, the incoming message brought a smile to her face. Lana stared at her, puzzled, when she realized what was bothering her. Daphne had her phone back. Priscilla had taken it off of her at the Museum of Bags and Purses. When had Daphne gotten it back? Had she asked the hotel staff to open her mother's room for her? *That must be it*, she reckoned, they wouldn't just toss out Priscilla's personal belongings, especially when her daughter was staying at the same hotel.

The young woman must have felt her staring, because Daphne looked up from her telephone and right at Lana. "Can I help you?"

"No, sorry, my mind is wandering. Excuse me," Lana apologized, then made a point of walking away from Daphne, towards Dotty and Sally. Luckily her boss was feeling better today, though still a bit tired. Sally doted on her, constantly asking whether she needed to sit down or take a drink of water.

"You are so good to me, Sally," Lana heard Dotty say. Lana watched the two friends, who were so comfortable in each other's company. Lana couldn't help but feel a bit jealous of their relationship and wonder why she and her own mother couldn't get along.

The Fantastic Four stuck together in a cluster at the front. Sara and Frieda's enthusiasm was contagious, and soon they were all oohing and aahing at the intricate displays of hyacinths, tulips, roses, and carnations. Lana was glad to see everyone getting along, when a loud shout broke the peace.

"Get away from me, will you?" Lana heard Daphne say. She turned around and saw Paige trailing behind Daphne, trying to asking a question. Whatever Paige wanted to know had brought clouds to the recent orphan's face. Daphne darted around Dotty and Sally in an attempt to get away from the writer. When Paige noticed the others watching their disagreement, she stopped chasing her prey, and that creepy smile settled on her face again.

Lana was surprised Paige was still on the tour, but the writer was determined to stay. She seemed to have a long list of questions for Daphne, but the recently orphaned woman clearly wasn't happy about it. Since Priscilla's death, Daphne had made a point of sticking with the group and sitting well away from Paige whenever possible.

Despite her evasive maneuvers, Paige was sticking to Daphne like glue. Whenever Daphne raised her eyes from her phone's screen, Paige jumped on her with a question about Priscilla's past. But it wasn't her professional life that interested the writer; it was Priscilla's parents, siblings, and first boyfriends that Paige wanted to know about. Daphne's irritation seemed to grow with every question. Lana was baffled. It seemed quite odd for Paige to keep pushing for information about Priscilla's younger years, especially when it was clear that Daphne was not going to help her out.

Given the tight deadline that Priscilla had mentioned and her untimely death, Lana would have expected Paige to stay at the hotel and focus on turning the material she had already gathered into a manuscript as quickly as possible. As twisted as it was, Priscilla's untimely death would only increase interest in her biography.

Thinking about Paige and Priscilla reminded Lana of the former CEO's strange late-night request. Priscilla had wanted to know which room Dotty was in, right after having a fight with either Daphne or Paige—Lana still was not certain which woman it was. Their high-pitched nasal voices were too similar.

When Daphne stormed off, Paige began to follow. Lana stepped in front of the writer, partly out of curiosity and partly to give the recently orphaned woman a break.

"Hey, Paige, how are you doing?" Lana asked, keeping her tone innocent.

Paige's brow furrowed as she tried to walk around Lana. Lana sidestepped in front of her. "Say, I've been meaning to ask you, are you planning on staying for the rest of the tour?"

"Why shouldn't I?" she asked, glaring up at Lana.

"Considering the subject of your biography is dead, I figured you would want to fly back to the States." Lana normally wouldn't have been so blunt with a guest, but the writer had only been added to the tour in order to interview Priscilla.

Paige laughed and looked ahead to where Daphne had gone. "There's plenty more to find out about Priscilla that would make for great exclusive material for the biography. She left a lot of money and property behind. Daphne hasn't come clean about a few details, but I am certain she will, if I keep at her. And when she does, her perfect new world will come crashing down. The drama isn't over yet, not for her."

"What are you talking about?" Lana was fed up with her mysterious insinuations.

"Did you know Priscilla had another child, one she gave up for adoption? That's why I kept pushing Priscilla about her younger years, because I wanted her to admit it. It would have been a great scoop for the book. But there is still a chance the child will come forward, now that Priscilla's death is a leading news story back home. I bet she or he will have a claim on Priscilla's possessions, which would put Daphne's dream life in jeopardy."

No wonder Daphne was not pleased to have Paige hounding her about this mystery child, Lana thought. Daphne must have realized that Paige wouldn't stop bothering her mother about it, until she came clean. Would Daphne have killed Priscilla, in order to keep this baby a secret so she could inherit everything? That was quite extreme, though her tours had taught Lana that anyone could be a killer, given the right circumstances.

"Think about it," Paige whispered. "Priscilla took away Daphne's chance at a promotion by forcing her to stay on as her personal assistant. Her salary is so low that Daphne still lives at home. And Priscilla disapproved so strongly of Daphne's latest boyfriend that she was going to disinherit her if Daphne continued seeing him. If anyone wanted Priscilla dead, it was Daphne. That windmill saved her from having to get her hands dirty."

When Lana stumbled in shock at Paige's accusations, the writer took the opportunity to speed walk towards Daphne. Not in the mood to chase after the woman, Lana let her go.

Because of her conversation with Paige, Lana hadn't noticed that her group was quite spread apart as they slowly walked through the wonderful gardens, trailing after their patient guide. Closest to her were Dotty and Sally, both admiring flower beds full of orange and purple tulips. Paige and Daphne were already quite far ahead. Lana saw her chance to find out more about Priscilla's late-night argument and her conversation with Dotty. She sprinted to catch up to her boss.

"Hi, ladies. Are you enjoying the gardens?"

"They are heavenly! How do those landscape designers think up all of the shapes and color combinations? They are true artists," Sally exclaimed.

"They sure are. Did you see the portrait of Vincent van Gogh made out of flowers? It's so realistic I swear you expect him to say hello," Dotty added.

Lana looked up the path, ensuring Daphne and Paige were too far away to hear their conversation. "Dotty, I hope you don't mind me asking, but Priscilla came to my room two nights ago and asked to speak to you. She had been arguing with someone and was pretty upset. What did she want from you?"

"I didn't know that she had been in an argument earlier in the evening. But Priscilla did ask—in confidence, mind you—if I could cancel the rest of Paige's reservations and book her on an earlier flight home."

"That's pretty extreme. Did she say why she wanted Paige to leave?"

"Not really. Only that some of the questions were unsettling and she was having trouble relaxing and enjoying her holiday with Daphne. I guess combining work and pleasure wasn't such a hot idea after all."

"But Priscilla didn't want to leave, only to send Paige home. Is that correct?"

"Yep. I told her I would book Paige on the next available flight home, if that's what she wanted. It was too late to cancel most of the hotel reservations and tours, but Priscilla wasn't concerned about getting a refund. She just wanted the writer off the tour as soon as possible."

"Did you tell the police this?"

"Why would I? I never did get the chance to change Paige's flight. And the police were only interested in knowing where we were when Priscilla fell. Besides, I don't think this has anything to do with her falling over. Unless –"

Dotty's mouth formed a tiny O. "Do you think Priscilla killed herself? That she was so upset by Paige's questions that she jumped off the balcony when Paige refused to leave?"

Dotty and Sally both covered their mouths with their hands.

"No, I wouldn't go that far."

Dotty grabbed her arm. "Do you think I should call the police and tell them, Lana?"

Lana considered her question. "No, I think you are right. That officer said the windmill's blade knocked Priscilla off the observation platform. It was an accident, which means Paige and Priscilla's fight wouldn't have any bearing on her death. Right?"

"I don't see how it could. But you're the investigator, not me."

"I *was* one, Dotty—long ago."

"You never know what the future holds, dear."

"That's true," Lana agreed, keeping her tone neutral. There was no reason to get in an argument over this with her boss. And right now Lana was too raw to really process her source's betrayal or the possibility that she could return to a career in journalism. Her thoughts turned again to Jeremy, when their guide stopped in the middle of the path and waited for them all to catch up.

"Ladies and gentleman, it has been my pleasure to show you the jewel of the Netherlands. We hope you enjoy the rest of your day."

The group clapped enthusiastically as he waved goodbye.

Lana started to head to the front, when Randy stepped forward. "We have an hour before our boat tour through the tulip fields begins. You can explore the park on your own, or we can stop and take a snack break. There is a wonderful café in the next greenhouse; it's around the corner and on the right."

Lana was impressed by how Randy handled himself. In Paris, admittedly his first tour as a Wanderlust guide, he had seemed so nervous and unsure. Lana was thrilled to see he was feeling more in control and confident.

"I could use a short break," Frieda called out. "This place is massive. I'll have to wear my gym shoes next time we go on a walking tour."

"I would rather take some more photos," Hadley piped up. Lana couldn't help but snort. Hadley had probably taken a thousand pictures this morning alone. If she wasn't taking selfies or photos of her mom, she was staging photos of her jewelry next to a tulip, or with the windmill in the background. She'd even asked a few of the ladies to hold up a bracelet or necklace so she could get a better angle on it. Lana couldn't figure out why she was so fond of her clunky bracelets.

"If you don't mind, Mom, I would rather walk around the gardens," Franny said. She was wearing enormous sunglasses that covered most of her face, but her height and perfect figure were impossible to hide. So far no one had recognized her by name, but Franny did receive appreciative glances from pretty much every male they passed.

Frieda nodded in approval. "That's fine, dear. It's your vacation, too."

Franny pecked her mother on the cheek, making Frieda blush like a schoolgirl.

"I'd rather wander around, too, Mom," Anne said.

Sara squeezed her arm. "You go enjoy yourself."

"Okay, gang, have fun, but do keep an eye on the time. Our boat ride through the tulip fields begins in an hour. We'll see you at the café in fifty minutes," Randy said.

As they walked away, Lana heard Franny say to Anne, "You looked great last night! I love your dance moves. I didn't expect to see you at the club."

Lana turned with a start. Maybe she had not imagined seeing Anne in clubbing clothes the other night. But why was she pretending to be such a stick in the mud when her mother was around? It didn't make any sense.

Before Anne could answer, Hadley sidled up to Franny.

"I just love your blouse, Francesca. The fabric would look really cool with this bracelet. Would you mind holding it up in front of that tulip for me?"

Lana examined Franny's clothes critically. The flowing fabric and Arabic-inspired pattern was gorgeous, but it was so busy and colorful that it didn't complement the jewelry at all.

Franny seemed surprised but recovered quickly. So far Hadley had been asking her advice about fashion or questions about her modeling career every chance she got. "Sure, why not?" She took the string of beads and did as Hadley asked.

Tammy watched the two women intently, a smile forming on her lips.

23

No Tiptoeing Through the Tulips

Just before they reached the café, their group passed a set of signs pointing to the various gardens and greenhouses spread throughout the Keukenhof.

Dotty exclaimed in delight, "Oh, the Princess Beatrix Pavilion is where they have all those orchids, isn't it, Sally? I thought that's what our guide said. I don't want to miss that. Are you game? Or would you rather take a coffee break?"

"Orchids are one of my favorites. I would love to join you."

The two knitting friends followed the arrow leading towards the greenhouse, already deep in conversation about the delicate plants and the care needed to maintain them.

"Okay, see you," Lana called out to their backs. She knew Dotty wasn't feeling up to snuff, but she had expected a little more attention from her boss, especially considering Priscilla's actions and her mother's betrayal.

Lana shook it off, choosing to focus on her guests instead of her hurt feelings. She and Randy settled the rest of their guests around one table in the café and took their orders. After the two guides distributed the first round of drinks, Randy pulled Lana aside.

"Do you mind if I took a few minutes for myself? I need to sort a few things out."

"Of course. Hey, you're doing a great job, but you do seem a bit restless. Is everything alright?"

Randy laughed as he pulled his fingers through his wavy red hair. "Is it that obvious? My brother, Alex, is in town for work and wants to get together tomorrow. With everything that happened yesterday, I forgot to book something for us to do."

"Oh, I'm sure he'll just be happy to see you." Lana said, relieved that there wasn't anything more traumatic going on in his life.

Randy looked away. "I, uh, also forgot to mention his coming to you."

Lana felt her stomach sink, dreading his next words. "How do I fit in the picture?"

"I know this is strange timing, but my brother is a great guy, and I think you should join us. I've told him all about you and think you two would really hit it off." Randy smiled encouragingly.

"Are you kidding me? No way! This tour is already difficult enough with Priscilla's death, my mom, and our argumentative guests. Please don't try to fix me up with someone right now," Lana pleaded.

Randy gazed at her with his droopy dog eyes. "Okay. It's too bad; we both travel so much for work that our paths hardly cross these days. And I really do think you two would get along well."

"Just like me and your climbing buddy did?" Lana teased. The last time Randy set her up, her date was so boring that Lana had kept ordering coffees just to stay awake.

"Okay, I'll admit that he wasn't a great choice. But my brother –"

Lana arched an eyebrow at him and crossed her arms.

Randy raised his palms in defeat. "Okay, I'll let it go—for now."

Lana chuckled. "Between you, Dotty, and Willow, I will never run out of potential suitors. Enjoy your walk. I'll see you in a half hour."

"Thanks, Lana," he said and strolled away.

When Lana returned to her guests, Tammy, Frieda, and Sara were all sitting with their hands folded into their laps and their heads tilted forward. Lana swore she could hear Tammy softly snoring. When Lana plopped down between Sara and Frieda, the ladies' eyes shot back open.

"So, Frieda, your daughter is a fashion model?" Lana asked, unable to keep her curiosity contained.

"I'm afraid so," her guest replied.

"I don't understand why you are so upset," Tammy said. "If my daughter was a top model, I would be telling everyone I met."

"Not if her lady parts were so exposed in all those pictures."

"Sex sells, doesn't it?" Tammy shrugged.

"Yeah, well, I would rather it wasn't my flesh and blood doing the selling," Frieda said as she stared Tammy down.

"Is that the only reason why you hate Franny's job, Frieda?" Sara asked.

"Prancing around on a catwalk isn't work. I don't care if those angel wings are heavy. Franny's got a great head on her shoulders. It's just too bad she's not using it. She graduated cum laude with a master's degree in business management, for goodness' sake! She should be climbing the corporate ladder and working on building up her pension. Lord knows she's got the brains to succeed."

"I don't know, some models make millions," Tammy added.

Frieda glared at her. "At what cost? All you hear are stories about rampant drug and alcohol abuse and how most of them are bulimics."

"Franny looks quite healthy to me. Did you see how muscular her arms are? If I need a jar opened, I know who to ask," Sara reasoned.

"I can't show any of her work photos to my male friends. One of my colleagues at my volunteer gig had a photo of Franny in a bikini as his screensaver. I was so embarrassed, I made him change it."

Sara and Tammy tittered with laughter.

Frieda glared at them, then continued. "And she's always on the road. Last month she was in Florida, Shanghai, and Australia. I never get to see her anymore."

Sara's mouth fell open. "Oh, my! She's seeing a lot more of the world than I ever did at her age. What an opportunity! I sure wish my Anne had the chance to do the same. Heck, I'd be happy if she traveled to the grocery store on her own, just to get her off my couch. I swear her backside has made a permanent dent in the cushions. Ever since she got fired and moved back in, all she does is surf online and watch daytime television."

"Has she seen *The Bold and the Beautiful*? The storyline is getting good."

"I'm not recommending your favorite soaps to Anne! I can't get her out of the house as it is. She's thirty-four years old, Frieda. She should be out there trying to rustle up more clients, not moping around my living room."

"At least you get to see your daughter."

Screams stopped their conversation in its tracks as they all looked around for the source. Seconds later, the café door burst open. A security guard had Hadley by the arm.

"Let me go!" she shrieked, as she squirmed in the bulky man's tight grip. The guard scanned the room and zeroed in on Lana, already jogging towards them.

"This young woman is part of my tour group. What is going on?"

"It is strictly forbidden to walk through the flower beds. Yet this young lady ignored all of posted signs and refused to heed our security guards' warnings. We had to physically remove her from the river of tulips."

Lana shook her head in disbelief. What was Hadley thinking? The girl was obsessed with getting just the right photo, regardless of the cost to others.

"Lana said I could go anywhere I wanted," Hadley whined.

"That's not what I meant. You can't ignore their rules," Lana scolded her.

"Get your hands off my daughter!" Tammy's cry echoed throughout the café as she lumbered over.

"Oh, Hadley, did he hurt you?" she asked when she finally reached them. Tammy slapped the security guard's arm until he released his grip on her daughter. She pulled Hadley close and scowled at the large man.

"We should sue you for mishandling and psychological damage! How dare you treat my daughter like a criminal, you brute!"

Hadley began weeping on her mother's shoulder.

Give them both an A for effort, Lana thought, as Tammy continued to berate the security guard. Unable to listen to her baseless accusations any longer, Lana broke in.

"Enough! Hadley was in the wrong. She was walking through the flower beds when the signs clearly state not to."

Hadley's bottom lip trembled. "Those photos were perfect for my social media, but he deleted them all."

"How dare you touch her work phone! That's got to be an invasion of privacy. I want your badge number," Tammy screeched.

"Your daughter destroyed several dozen flowers. Those plants are the farmers' livelihoods; they aren't props for your photographs," the guard stated.

"I am so sorry for causing you trouble," Lana added when Tammy remained silent. She pulled out her wallet. "How much do we owe you?"

He waved away her offer. "Just keep your guests out of the flower beds, please."

"It won't happen again, I promise."

He nodded and wished Lana well, glaring at Hadley once more for good measure before he left.

"At least I was able to post one photo online before the guards got to me," Hadley said. "My number of followers is going to go through the roof."

24

A Living Rainbow

By the time Randy returned to the café, the rest of the guests had arrived, and their group was complete once again.

"I've never seen so many varieties of orchids," Dotty enthused while showing Lana several photos of the plants.

"Their branches are so delicate! They don't even look strong enough to hold those gigantic flowers," Sally added.

"They sure are pretty," Lana said. "I do love the colors. I've never seen such a deep purple before."

Randy moved to the front of the group and cleared his throat. "Okay, gang, next up is our boat ride through the tulip fields. Is everyone ready to go?"

"I can't wait for this one. I bet I'll get a few hundred extra followers just from the boat ride alone," Hadley said.

Lana wondered, yet again, why social media was so important to Hadley.

"Great! Let's go," Randy said before leading the way to the boat rentals. They wound their way along the tree-lined paths to a historic windmill at the edge of the park. Behind it were the colorful flower fields they would be sailing through. Lana shivered as she thought about Priscilla and wondered how seeing the windmill would affect Daphne. Lana's heart went out to the recently orphaned woman, until she noticed that Daphne was still glued to her phone. The smile on her face led Lana to believe that she was chatting with her boyfriend again.

Close to the base of the windmill was a line of little aluminum boats. Each boat could hold up to five tourists and the captain. Lana was glad to see these were skippered. Wanderlust Tours had reserved three of them. As soon as Frieda and Franny climbed into the first boat, Hadley and Tammy sprung aboard before Sara and Anne could.

When Frieda started to protest, saying she wanted to ride with her friend, Sara said, "It's no bother. This way we can take pictures of each other while we're sailing."

"That's a great point," Frieda said and settled in next to her daughter and across from Tammy.

After Sara and Anne climbed into the second boat, Dotty asked, "Can we sit with you? Sally and I haven't had much of a chance to chat with you two since the tour started. Are you enjoying it so far?"

"Oh, yes," Sara exclaimed. "Between the fancy hotels and interesting day trips, your Wanderlust tours always keep us entertained. And I do like the mother-daughter theme," she said, wrapping an arm around Anne's waist. "It's a great excuse to go on vacation together, isn't it?"

Anne smiled politely, but otherwise seemed uninterested in making small talk.

Paige watched Daphne, who was clearly struggling to figure out where to sit, when the recently orphaned woman sprung into Frieda's boat. Paige started to board it too, when the captain said, "I am sorry, miss, this boat is full."

Paige glared at Daphne, who shot her a nasty look in return, then boarded the second boat and sat next to Anne.

Lana climbed into the third boat, next to Randy. "It's just the two of us. I guess we're off the clock for the next hour," she teased, hoping he wouldn't use the time to try to persuade her to meet up with his brother.

Their captains pushed off, and the three boats joined a line of others traversing the narrow canals crisscrossing the long fields. Lana took in the explosions of color, marveling in the richness of the reds, pinks, purples, yellows, and oranges. Because so many blossoms of the same color were grown close together, the hues seemed to be deeper and richer than normal.

It was quite serene sailing around the fields like this. The broad swathes of bright colors looked like a living rainbow, and floating through the flowers at eye level was magical.

"How are you doing, Lana?" Randy asked. "We haven't had a chance to talk since Priscilla's accident."

"That's a great question," she responded. "Today's tour has been a welcome distraction, but at some point I'm going to have to deal with my mother."

"If you want to skip the dinner tonight, just let me know. I figured you'd need time to sort out your feelings. Dotty told me about what Gillian did. I am truly sorry. That's got to hurt."

Lana's laugh was a bitter one. "Yeah, you could say that."

"Dotty also told me that it was a business decision, not a personal attack."

"Well, that's what my mom claims. I'm going to get in touch with her assistant to find out for myself, when my head is in the right space. Right now, I'm still too hurt to care if she knew or not."

Randy nodded. "Fair enough. It's probably better to steer clear from Gillian now. You don't want to say something you'll later regret."

"I guess you're right. I just wish Dotty hadn't invited her."

"What are you planning on doing during your free time tomorrow?" he asked, clearly trying to change to subject.

Their group had a free morning and afternoon to do whatever they wished, which meant she and Randy had the day off, as well. Several of their clients had already booked bike and walking tours, though Dotty and Sally preferred to visit a certain museum and had invited Lana to come along.

"Dotty mentioned the Cat Cabinet. I'm thinking of joining her and Sally." Lana braced for a comment about how she should spend her time with Gillian. Luckily, Randy didn't go there.

"Did you say Cat Cabinet? What the heck is that?"

"It's a museum dedicated to artwork featuring cats."

"That sounds right up Dotty's alley." Randy laughed.

Lana chuckled along, reveling in the sunshine and beautiful views. As the canal widened, the three boats' captains brought them closer together so that Frieda and Sara could take pictures of each other with the tulips in the background.

"That's gorgeous," Frieda called out as she checked the pictures she had just taken of Sara and Anne. "Take a few of Franny and me with the purple tulips in the background. Those are my favorites," she yelled over to her friend.

After Sara did as asked, Hadley removed several bracelets from her wrists.

Here we go again, Lana thought. How many photos of her jewelry did that girl need to take?

"Frieda, would you mind holding my bracelets for a photo? The yellow tulips behind you are so striking. It would be a great shot," she said.

Lana knew that Frieda wasn't too keen on Hadley or Tammy, but she was also too polite to say no. "Alright then. Is this good?"

"Try holding them so they dangle off of your fingertips. Spread your palm out a bit more. Perfect." Once she'd taken several, she grinned at Frieda and took back her jewelry. "Thanks a million. Those are perfect."

"What is it you do, Hadley? Are you a photographer?" Frieda asked.

"Hadley's a social media influencer," Tammy said proudly.

"A what?"

"She has a popular blog where she shares her shopping tips. She has seven million followers on Instagram. Can you believe it? That's probably more than your Francesca has!"

Lana was mortified, but Franny took it all in stride. "You're right, that's way more than I have."

Hadley puffed up with pride. "I share my tips for finding treasures in secondhand stores, as well as ways to alter the garments so they are hip again."

That explained the clothing and the hounding of Franny for fashion advice, Lana realized.

"More and more thrift store owners are reaching out, asking me to feature their shop on my blog."

"Some of them even pay her hundreds of dollars to post about them. Can you believe it?" Tammy added.

Lana's eyebrows shot up. She had no idea influencers like Hadley could make so much money off of their social media accounts.

"Hadley is so creative," her mother gushed. "She recently started making these necklaces and bracelets. They are selling really well online. Since I can't assist her financially, I'm helping her get them into local shops," Tammy added.

So Hadley made them! Her obsession with photographing those beaded creations now made perfect sense. Still, Lana was shocked to hear her jewelry was selling well. *It must be the sheer number of followers*, Lana thought.

"How much do you charge for one bracelet?" Frieda asked.

"Fifty-nine dollars. And double for the necklaces."

Lana choked, then pretended to cough into her hand. "That is quite impressive, Hadley," she said diplomatically.

The young woman smiled in response.

The canal narrowed, and their boats once again pulled behind each other, like ducks in a row. They slowly puttered their way back to the windmill in the Keukenhof Gardens. After an hour of floating amongst the tulip fields on this sunny spring day, they were all relaxed and satisfied when they returned to the dock.

Her guests chatted pleasantly as they walked back to their waiting bus. Lana was grateful for a day with no major squabbling. After Priscilla's tragic death, Lana hadn't been certain the tour would be able to go on. Perhaps it wasn't doomed, just yet.

25

The Other Miss Hansen

When her group got back to the hotel, all Lana wanted to do was collapse on her bed. Their dinner at the traditional Dutch restaurant d'Vijff Vlieghen had been delicious, and she had overeaten again. Lana knew she should go talk to her mother, grown-up to grown-up. But she just wasn't up to it.

"Tomorrow," Lana mumbled to herself, as she stood before her door, fishing around her purse for her room key.

"Miss Hansen?" a booming voice asked.

Lost in thought, Lana hadn't heard the man approaching. Startled, she turned around to find the police inspector from the windmill standing before her.

"Yes?"

He looked at her in confusion. "Oh, you're the tour guide from Zaanse Schans. The receptionist must have made a mistake. You are not the Miss Hansen I am looking for. Do you know which room Gillian Hansen is in?"

"Yes, she is in room 29, further up the hallway on the right." Lana said, pointing the way.

"Thank you and good night," the officer said and turned to leave.

"Wait a moment, why do you want to talk to my mother?"

"Your mother?" His eyes narrowed as he considered his answer. After a long silence, he said, "To see if she can clarify something for us."

Lana put her hands on her hips. "What do you mean exactly? Does she need a lawyer? Should I be present?"

"No, not at this time," he said. His smile was clearly meant to appease Lana, but it didn't work.

"We have taken statements from all of the tourists at the windmill yesterday afternoon, and there is some confusion as to where exactly your mother was when Priscilla Andersen fell. Gillian Hansen was wearing a striking outfit, one that many tourists recall seeing."

That's one way of putting it, Lana thought. Her mother had always had an affection for designer outfits in shockingly bright colors. She and Gillian both had the skin tone and figure to pull them off, but Lana would never be caught dead in the vivid colors that her mother favored.

"Now if you will excuse me, I wish to speak to Ms. Hansen so I can complete my duties for the day and then go home to my wife," he added when Lana made no move to open her door.

"Of course, have a good night," she said before pulling her key out of her bag.

As she opened her door, she heard another door closing.

Oh no, she thought, *did one of the guests hear my conversation with the inspector?* That was all she needed—for one of the others to think that Gillian was somehow involved in Priscilla's untimely death.

26

In Need of Legal Advice

May 6—Day Five of the Wanderlust Tour in Amsterdam

Lana woke with a start, momentarily confused as to where she was at. Horrible nightmares involving her mother had dominated her dreams, leaving her feeling drained and lethargic. Knowing that today was their group's free day was the only reason she got out of bed.

Getting through the Keukenhof tour and dinner last night had sapped her energy. Luckily, she and Randy wouldn't have to play guide until this evening when their group met up for a candlelight dinner cruise. All she had to do was get through breakfast.

When Lana stumbled into the bathroom, she grimaced at the zombie woman staring back at her in the mirror. The circles under her eyes were deep purple, and her skin was blotchy from crying. After a long, hot shower, Lana applied more makeup than usual. Unfortunately the foundation did little to hide the irregularities in her skin tone.

With a resigned sigh, Lana tossed her makeup bag aside and headed downstairs.

Randy was already in the breakfast room serving coffee when Lana entered. After breakfast, they would ensure the guests who had booked optional tours got into the right taxi or bus, then they were free to do whatever they wanted.

As much as Lana would have preferred to duck back under her covers,

Dotty had already talked her into visiting the Cat Cabinet with her and Sally today. Lana was certain Gillian was also invited.

She picked up a plate, wanting to fuel up before dealing with her guests, when Franny's rising voice drew her attention.

"You have got to be joking!" The model rushed over to Hadley and thrust her phone into the blogger's face. "What are you playing at?"

Frieda stood up and joined Franny. "What's going on?"

"Hadley posted a photo of me holding one of her bracelets to her Instagram account! And she had the nerve to tag me in it."

"Why shouldn't she tag you? You're in the photo," Tammy replied, as if Franny was a fool for asking.

Both Frieda's and Franny's mouths dropped open. "How could you post a photo of my daughter, one meant to help advertise your business, and think that she would approve? Companies pay Franny thousands of dollars to promote their products."

"She's a public figure who happened to be holding one of my designs. I didn't hire Francesca to model my bracelets," Hadley responded, avoiding Franny's glare.

"No, you didn't—nor did you ask my permission," the model countered.

"You would have said no," Hadley said dismissively, finally making eye contact with Franny.

"Unbelievable!" Frieda exclaimed. "You have no scruples, young lady. You took a photo during a private moment and turned it into a marketing campaign. If you don't take it down now, I'm going to contact my lawyer," she yelled.

"Don't worry, Mom. I have one on retainer who specializes in this sort of case," Franny said.

"You spoiled fat cats are all the same!" Tammy shrieked. She bunched up her fists and started bouncing on her heels. Lana was afraid she might actually strike Franny. Randy must have thought so, too, because he stood up and placed himself between the two sets of mothers and daughters.

"Ladies, why don't we all take our seats. This is your vacation, remember?"

"You and are your mother are just as bad as Priscilla," Tammy continued her tirade, her face turning a darker shade of burgundy the longer she blustered on. "Why can't you show any empathy for the little people who are trying to make a living, too?"

"Whoa! Ladies, let's take it down a notch," Lana said. She turned to Tammy and Hadley. "I don't know much about this sort of thing, but it sure seems fishy, you posting that photo on a social media account you're making money off of. Francesca is not here to work; she is here on vacation with her mother. You should respect her privacy."

"You're right; you don't know what you're talking about," Tammy retorted. "Go ahead and call your lawyer, Franny. Until we are forced to take it down, you are going to stay on Hadley's social media accounts."

The model held up her phone. "You asked for it." She waved her mother back to their seats as she called a number on speed dial.

Curiosity got the better of Lana. She quickly navigated to Instagram and looked up Hadley's account. The photos were a combination of well-framed travel shots and selfies, as well as close-ups of her jewelry. In her latest post, Franny held up a bracelet in front of a flower bed full of red tulips. Hadley had framed it so that Franny was the focus, not her jewelry. Lana could understand why the model was so upset.

A few moments later, Lana could hear Franny talking with someone. When the model rose and approached Tammy's table again, her smile was smug. "It's Tammy, correct? What is your last name and telephone number? That will speed up the process."

Tammy snorted but didn't turn around to face her. "Your lawyer can figure it out. I'm sure you're paying him enough."

Before Franny could respond, Dotty waved her over. Lana followed the model to her boss's table, luckily on the other side of the room.

When Franny was close enough, Dotty whispered, "Don't worry, Franny. I always carry a list of our guests' contact information with me." She searched around in her large purse until she found a folded sheet of paper.

Lana was relieved Dotty was here and had offered. She would not have felt comfortable sharing another guest's contact information without Dotty's explicit approval.

Franny scanned the list of names and numbers before reciting one to her lawyer.

Moments later, Tammy's phone began to beep. When she looked at the screen, she cackled. "I just received a cease-and-desist letter from Francesca's lawyer. That was in record time."

"You'd better take the photo down before we have to pay a fine," she snapped in Hadley's direction while throwing Franny a look that made Lana momentarily frightened for the model.

Based on their reactions, Lana suspected this wasn't the first time Tammy and Hadley had tried the same trick. As she watched Hadley delete the photo, Lana thought, *What a devious duo.*

27

Finding Love in Unexpected Places

After the chaotic breakfast, Lana's guests were eager to get their day started. Once they'd all been sent on their way, Lana walked to the lobby to ask the receptionist whether she could recommend a lunch café that was close to the Cat Cabinet.

There was a short line of travelers waiting to ask questions and check in. Lana waited patiently for her turn. Once the receptionist offered a few suggestions and marked them on a map, Lana thanked the woman and examined her options. All were short walks from the museum, she noticed, turning from the desk—map in hand—her concentration focused on the street names they would need to look out for.

Lana took two steps and bonked into something solid.

"Watch out!"

She blushed automatically, realizing she had just walked into a guest waiting in line. A fan of paperwork covered the ground. Lana groaned, realizing she'd managed to knock the stranger's briefcase open.

"Oh, no, I'm so sorry," Lana babbled and knelt down to grab a handful of papers before rising to return them to their owner. When she stood up to hand them to the man, Lana heard angels sing as they made eye contact. The ruggedly attractive man before her had wavy reddish-brown hair, gentle eyes, and a gorgeous smile that drew her in.

She held out the papers, unable to speak.

When the tall stranger took them from her, their hands met, and Lana swore she felt a jolt of electricity.

"Thank you. I have got to get that lock fixed," he said. "The darn thing keeps bursting open at the most inopportune times." When he looked her up and down, his smile made her heart melt. "Though I have to say, I'm not sorry it did this time."

He stretched out his hand. "I'm Alex. And you are?"

"Ah…" Lana had never been so tongue-tied in her life. Feeling like a fool, she tried to string together a rational sentence, but one look into the man's sapphire eyes and her mind went blank.

Before Lana could recover, Randy entered the lobby.

"Hey, Alex!" he called out as he crossed over to them. "That's a great coincidence. I see you met Lana."

Alex's eyes widened, and his smile intensified. "You're Lana Hansen? It is a real pleasure to meet you. Randy's told me so much about you, I feel as if we've already met."

"Oh, you're Randy's brother? It's great to meet you, too. Randy mentioned you were in town. Are you here on business?" she asked as she slowly regained her ability to converse normally.

"Yes, for a training session. Say, Randy and I are going for a bike ride. Would you join us?"

"Yes, yes I would," Lana said, her eyes never leaving Alex's baby blues. "But I wouldn't want to intrude on your family time."

"It's no intrusion. I would love it if you joined us. You don't mind, do you, baby brother?" Alex asked, keeping his gaze fixed on Lana.

"Of course not," Randy said. "You know, I can take a rain check on the bike ride, if you and Lana would rather…"

"Don't be silly! Alex is here to see you, Randy," Lana insisted, finally tearing her gaze from Alex to make eye contact with her fellow guide.

With their spell broken, Alex turned to his brother and wrapped him up in a hug. "It's great to see you, little brother."

"You, too, Alex. But would you mind just calling me Randy when we're around the guests?"

"Sure, sorry about that. I forgot that you're on the clock."

"Let me rent another bike and then we can head out," Randy said.

"That sounds great," Lana replied. "But I need to let Dotty know I won't be joining her today. Do you mind waiting for me? I won't be but a minute."

"Sure, take your time. We'll wait for you here," Alex said. His smile motivated Lana to skip steps in her race to Dotty's room. Her pounding fist brought her boss to the door immediately.

"What is there, child? You just about gave me a heart attack!"

"Sorry, it's just—I can't join you today," Lana panted and shoved the map with lunch suggestions into Dotty's hand.

"Why on earth not? You and Gillian are never going to patch things up if you don't spend time together."

"It's not her, it's just—Randy's brother is here, and they invited me to go bike riding with them." Lana felt like a teenager asking her mother's permission to stay out late.

Dotty's frown disappeared in a heartbeat. "Oh, so Alex did make it? That's wonderful! You go have fun with him. Don't worry about Gillian. Sally and I will take real good care of her."

Lana's head spun at Dotty's quick reversal. "Wait a second; are you and Randy teaming up on me? Did Alex really come to Amsterdam just to meet me?"

"Well, and to see Randy. Alex is on the road a lot but was coincidentally in Holland for work this week. Alex wasn't sure if he could make it to Amsterdam, but when Randy told him that you would be here, he said he would do his best to make it happen. I'm glad he did. Alex is quite the catch," Dotty tittered, then closed the door before Lana could respond.

"I wonder what the catch is," Lana grumbled, as she ran back down to the lobby. One look at Alex made her realize it didn't matter. She was already smitten.

They set off by bike, letting Randy take the lead. They pedaled along the ringed canals in the center before crisscrossing through the Jordaan, which, according to her guidebooks, was formerly a working-class neighborhood but now a desired address. Lana enjoyed weaving through the narrow streets and compact houses, many with fake tulips and embroidered screens in their windows.

Alex and Lana chatted easily, sharing bits about their lives as they biked. Lana told Alex about her work as a magician's assistant and now guide. Alex explained how he gave workshops and training sessions at large corporations around Europe. He was home in Seattle for about six months, and the rest of the year he was on the road.

No wonder he and Randy had a hard time meeting up, she thought. A sudden realization made her lose her concentration, and she almost hit another cyclist. If he and Randy rarely saw each other, how often would she see him, if they began dating? Lana mentally slapped herself the second the thought entered her brain. She and Alex had just met; it was probably too soon to start worrying about their future together.

Lana forced herself to stay in the moment, reveling in the feeling of biking through the historic center of Amsterdam. It was magical pedaling over the old bridges and sneaking peeks into the manicured gardens hidden behind many of the tall, narrow canal houses. A plethora of brightly colored flowers filled the many planters hanging off of the bridges, streetlamps, and balconies.

Randy circled back to a main street, and then they were back on the canals, passing the Westerkerk, a gigantic church in the heart of the city center. Its dark tower, with a giant gold crown topping it, stood like a beacon on the outskirts of the Jordaan. Around its base snaked a line of tourists waiting to visit the Anne Frank House, just a few doors down.

They passed another church with a squat tower and thriving market around its base, then crossed through a tunnel and over a bridge. Their path brought them to Centraal Station. Moored next to the entrance was a boat completely filled with bicycles. Lana stopped to gape at the parking garage for two-wheelers, marveling at the sheer number. Behind the station, the views across the River IJ were magnificent. Ferry boats, barges, and a cruise ship all ploughed the choppy waters, while dinghies and tour boats weaved in between.

After they had circled behind the train station, Randy steered them towards a path along the waterfront. In the distance was the Basilica of Saint Nicholas, a church Lana recognized from her guidebooks thanks to the gigantic and richly decorated twin towers and dome soaring above the entrance. They biked towards a floating Chinese restaurant that dominated the harbor. Towering behind it were sleek skyscrapers, several advertising restaurants with panoramic views. In the distance was a strange green building, its shape reminiscent of a half-sunken ship.

"There's a bike path back here I want to check out," Randy called out as he navigated onto a small path that led to a narrow bridge. On the other side was a cube-shaped building tilted so it appeared to be balancing on one corner.

As they got closer, Alex began to laugh. "Climbing Amsterdam, huh?"

"That's serendipitous," Randy said, having trouble keeping a straight face.

Alex laughed. "Knowing you, little brother, this was a setup!"

Lana laughed along, thinking, *In more ways than one.*

"What do you think, Lana?" Alex asked. "Would you like to do some rock climbing?"

Lana's head began bobbing in affirmation before her mind could register what he had just asked. When his words sunk in, Lana immediately regretted saying yes. She hadn't rock climbed since her dad died. And even then, she had only dabbled in it. Unlike her father, she had never really felt comfortable in the harness.

"Have you climbed before, Lana?" Randy asked.

"Yes, but it's been more than twenty years." Lana thought back on her father. He had taught her how to climb, but it had never become her passion, as it was his. Still, she treasured their time together and would never forget her dad's patience and encouragement.

"It's like riding a bike. Once you learn, you don't really ever forget," Randy said.

"And we're here to help," Alex added.

Lana looked up at Alex, so caring and sincere, and wanted to pinch herself. After months of wondering whether she would ever find love again, the perfect man showed up out of nowhere.

Once they entered the funky building and saw the climbing routes, Lana felt the familiar rush of adrenaline and nausea. Despite being tied to a rope the entire time, Lana couldn't shake the feeling that she could fall at any moment. When she had trouble getting into her harness, Alex helped her, gently adjusting the straps so it fit properly.

Her first time up was embarrassing, to say the least. Yet once she got the hang of it again and actually made contact with the footholds instead of sliding off of them, she was able to climb to the top of the easiest route. She had also forgotten what a workout it was, as she pushed and heaved with all her might, reveling in her burning muscles and panting lungs.

Once she touched the top, Alex and Randy began cheering. When she belayed down to the ground, Alex leaned in and gave her a spontaneous kiss on the cheek. It took all of Lana's self-control not to wrap her arms around his neck and kiss him back.

Based on Randy's never-ending grin, he was pleased to see the two of them getting along.

When Alex began ascending the more difficult route, Lana's protective self-doubt began making her question him and his motives. Lana moved closer to Randy, who was holding onto his brother's rope, and asked, "So what's the catch?"

"What do you mean?"

"Your brother seems perfect. Why isn't he happily married with kids?"

Randy grew visibly uncomfortable. "He should probably tell you himself."

"Randy, I've been burned too many times. If there's something I should know about, you need to tell me now, before I fall hard for the guy. As a friend and co-worker."

"He's recently divorced, just like you."

"What happened?"

Randy was silent for a moment, before finally explaining, "Alex came home early from a business trip and found his wife in bed with another man. Apparently she was sick of him being on the road all the time and decided to cheat on him, instead of talking to him about it."

"That must have really hurt." Lana thought back to the horrible shock she'd experienced when reading her ex-husband's text message telling her their marriage was over. She couldn't imagine the pain and anger she would have felt if she'd actually caught her ex and his assistant in bed together.

"Thanks for telling me. I really appreciate knowing."

"After what Ron did to you, I figured you would understand," Randy said.

As she watched Alex climb nimbly up the wall, Lana was once again reminded of her father. He would have been so proud of her today. She hadn't climbed in so long that simply being here reminded her of him in an overpowering way. She missed her dad terribly. So far, Alex reminded her of her father.

Lana could never forget that one of their last conversations was a silly argument. Her dad had been adamant that she attend a state university to save money, while she'd been determined to attend the best journalism school in the country, instead. How she regretted that fight and wished she'd given in, if only to appease him.

Thoughts of her father turned to her mother. What about Gillian? If she didn't forgive her now, they would never reconnect, but drift apart forever. And Lana's last memory of her mother would also be a horrible argument.

Lana was content to let the police investigate Priscilla's death and assumed they would soon realize Gillian didn't do it. But what if they didn't find any other viable suspects? Gillian and Priscilla were both powerful, respected businesswomen back home, but here they were just two American tourists. Were the Dutch police even capable of investigating Priscilla's death as thoroughly as the Seattle police could?

If Lana wanted to see her mother go free, she would have to find out more about her guests and their connections to Priscilla. If the former CEO had been murdered, her killer was most likely a guest on Lana's tour.

As painful as learning the truth about Hansen Advertising's work for McGruffin Wood had been, she was glad it was now out in the open so they could try to patch things up. Yet before she could truly forgive Gillian, she needed to know how involved her mother had been with the McGruffin account. After they were done climbing, she would call Gillian's assistant, Lana decided.

Moments later, Alex reached the top, yelling out in delight. Randy and Lana cheered for him as he belayed back down. When he touched the ground, Lana sprung forward and kissed him lightly on the lips. His surprise made her hesitate, wondering if she'd gone too far, when he grabbed her tight and kissed her back. Calls of "get a room" from customers waiting in line to climb broke their spell.

Lana blushed as they pulled apart. She couldn't help but marvel at life's little ironies. Here she was, at one of the lowest points in her life, and yet she'd met the man of her dreams.

After they had turned in their gear, Alex and Lana shared a strawberry and kiwi smoothie before the three of them headed back to the hotel. On their ride back, Alex rode next to Lana chatting the whole way. Randy was unusually quiet, seemingly content to see his brother and Lana happy together.

Lana had not felt this comfortable around a potential suitor in such a long time that when they reached the hotel, she had trouble saying goodbye. All Lana wanted to do was spend time with Alex, but duty called. In an hour, they had to meet their group in the lobby and accompany them to dinner.

Randy must have noticed that both Alex and Lana were having trouble parting ways, too. After he'd collected their bike keys, he said softly to Lana, "You know, Dotty is feeling better and will be joining us for dinner. Why don't you take the night off?"

Lana wanted to jump with joy. Randy must have read her mind!

"That sounds wonderful," she whispered back, keeping her tone even. His brother was standing right next to them.

Lana turned to Alex and said shyly, "Would you like to have dinner with me?"

He took her hand and kissed it, his eyes locked on hers the whole time. "Yes, I would like that very much."

His smile melted Lana's heart.

28

Lies and Conjecture

After a wonderful dinner, a walk along the canals, and a nightcap, Lana was in seventh heaven. Alex was kind, considerate, funny, attentive—and sexy to boot. Lana had never fallen this quickly for someone, and from the looks of it, Alex was just as keen on her.

Arm in arm, they walked back up to Lana's hotel room. The day had gone so perfectly, but she still wasn't certain whether it was wise to invite him into her room. A few doors away, Alex pushed her up against the wall and kissed her passionately. After that, Lana didn't care whether it was wise; she couldn't wait to get him inside and see what happened.

All of sudden, Alex released her and took a step back. Lana looked at him in confusion when his eyes shot to the left. Lana jumped a foot in the air when she realized Hadley was standing right next to them with her arms crossed over her torso.

Lana wiped her mouth off with the back of her hand, then smoothed her dress down. "Hadley, what can I do for you?"

Why didn't she go find Randy if she had a question? Lana wondered. *He's the one on duty right now.*

"Gillian is your mother, right?" Hadley asked.

"Yes."

"We need to talk," Hadley said, glaring at Alex as she added, "Alone."

Oh no, did she get in a fight with Gillian? Lana wondered, hoping whatever it was wouldn't take long.

"Okay, Hadley. Sure. Um, Alex, I'll, ah, be in touch soon?"

"Sure, I'll call you as soon as I know when I'll be back in Amsterdam," Alex said, seeming equally disappointed by Hadley's interruption. He pecked her on the cheek, then sauntered back to his room. Lana knew he was taking an early morning train to Eindhoven. Luckily he'd already offered to come back to Amsterdam after his training session wrapped up, so they could spend a few more hours together before she flew home. Still, this was not how she'd hoped this day would end.

After he'd walked out of sight, Lana found her room key and opened her door. Hadley shoved her way inside.

"Shut that door. You won't want anyone to hear this."

Lana was too stunned to disobey. She closed the door, asking, "What is there, Hadley?"

"I was going through my photos of Zaanse Schans for a blog post when I found some incriminating photos of your mother. She's standing out on the windmill's balcony right before Priscilla died. I can show them to the police, and Gillian will be arrested. Or you can pay me ten thousand dollars and I delete them all. It's your choice."

Lana was dumbfounded. "Wait, what do you mean, incriminating photos? Gillian never denied being out on that platform right before Priscilla died."

"Oh yeah? She told the police she was trying to get down the stairs when Priscilla fell. Take a look yourself and tell me what you see."

Hadley held her phone up so Lana could see the photos. Visible in the corner of each image was the time and date. She slowly flipped through several shots of the windmill taken in quick succession. In the first shot, Lana's hands were around Priscilla's throat. She blushed in embarrassment as her feeling of helplessness returned. In the next frame, Lana was stepping away from Priscilla, and Gillian was standing just behind them. In the third photo, Lana was running away, but neither Priscilla nor Gillian had moved. A frame later, Gillian was now turned towards Priscilla and was standing quite close to the former CEO. When Hadley flipped to the following picture, Gillian was slightly blurry, as if she was charging towards Priscilla.

"Pay attention to the time difference between these last two shots. It's only eleven seconds."

When Hadley showed her the next shot, indeed taken eleven seconds later, a blur passed in front of the camera. It was Priscilla's body falling towards the earth.

Oh, no, Gillian did push Priscilla over the edge, Lana moaned internally. Gillian had sworn she hadn't harmed the former CEO and that she'd been waiting to descend the stairs when Priscilla fell. She instinctively reached out for the phone to snatch it out of Hadley's hand.

Hadley jerked it away and waggled a finger at her. "Don't touch. Even if you delete these, I already forwarded all of the photos to my mom."

"What do you want?"

"I told you, money. You bring me ten grand, and I'll forget I ever took them."

"The police aren't going to arrest Gillian on the basis of these."

"Maybe, maybe not. I don't know if you want to take that chance. I heard you talking to the investigator last night in the hallway. He was looking for your mom. If the police have already figured out that Gillian was lying about where she was when Priscilla fell, they will be quite receptive to these photos. Besides, Priscilla was wealthy; I bet her family will pay a reward for the capture of her murderer."

"She fell. No one killed her," Lana stated.

"If you won't pay me, then we will see what the cops think," Hadley said dismissively.

Lana laughed, but she watched Hadley warily. The girl was dangerous. "Think this through, Hadley. A photo of my mom and Priscilla doesn't prove anything. Everyone knows they were both up on the balcony right before Priscilla fell. If anyone killed her, it was probably your mother. Tammy was the one who threatened Priscilla and had far more reason to want her dead than Gillian did. And your mom was out on the observation deck when Priscilla fell, too."

"Don't you dare try to pin this on my mom!" Hadley cried. "Your mom did it, not mine. We'll see what the police think when they see the time stamp. I bet this was the last photo of Priscilla taken before Gillian pushed her over the edge."

"You are completely insane. That's all lies and conjecture; those photos are not definitive proof."

Hadley pushed past Lana and raced out of her hotel room.

Lana picked up the phone, then replaced the receiver when she realized she didn't know who to call. Would Hadley actually go to the police? Lana shook her head. No, Tammy's motives for harming Priscilla were far stronger, Lana reckoned, when a twinge of doubt entered her brain.

Did her mother have a motive to harm Priscilla? Lana still hadn't had a chance to talk to Gillian since their last confrontation the night Priscilla died. Had Gillian shoved Priscilla into the windmill's blade? If yes, had it been accidental or intentional? Lana had been so emotional while running away from Priscilla that she had been completely unaware of who was around her.

But why would her mom want to harm Priscilla? She wouldn't have had a reason to, unless something significant did happen when her agency was working for McGruffin and Gillian didn't want Lana to find out about it.

But would her mother really kill someone to prevent them from talking? She and Gillian didn't always get along, but Lana couldn't believe that her mother was so cold-blooded.

Lana considered the possibility that Gillian was a killer for a moment. No matter how mad she was at her mother, Lana was certain she was not a murderer. However, she did need to speak to Gillian, and fast. Hadley's confidence and heartlessness made her a loose cannon, and she didn't want Gillian to find out about the windmill photos in the same way she had.

Lana dropped her coat on the bed and headed back out into the hallway.

29

It's All a Blur

"Lana, are you alright?" Gillian asked. "It's after midnight. What's wrong?"

"Can I come in?" Lana asked, whispering so her voice didn't carry down the hotel's hallway. If Hadley or Tammy saw Lana talking to her mother now, it might lead them to believe there was more to the photos than simply an unfortunate perspective. The last thing she wanted to be doing right now was talking to Gillian, but Hadley's photos demanded it. The girl was so unstable, Lana was certain she would try to blackmail Gillian, in person this time. As much as her mother had hurt her, Lana couldn't with a good conscience allow Hadley to surprise her with this.

"Of course." Gillian stepped back so her daughter could enter.

As soon as the door was firmly closed, Lana asked, "Mom, what exactly happened up on the windmill's deck after I ran away from Priscilla?"

Gillian looked at her through slitted eyes, as if she was concerned Lana was wearing a wire. "Why do you want to know?"

In her bathrobe, with no makeup on and messy hair, Gillian looked so vulnerable. Lana almost felt bad having to tell her the truth.

"Because Hadley just came to my room and showed me a series of photos she took of the windmill, from the ground. In the last two, it looks like you are moving in to strike Priscilla, and then she's falling over the edge of the railing. They were taken eleven seconds apart, and no one else is visible in either photograph."

Gillian sat heavily onto her bed and stared at her hands. "Oh, Lana, it's all a blur. After I pulled you off of Priscilla and you ran away, I was so mad at her. I recall telling her off before I ran after you, but it was in the heat of the moment. My gestures may have been suggestive of violence, but I assure you, I have never slapped or hit anyone in a fit of anger."

Lana reddened, remembering how good it had felt to have Priscilla's throat in between her hands, and how she would have gladly crushed the woman's windpipe if her mother hadn't stepped in.

"Was anyone else from our group still up there?"

Gillian's forehead creased in concentration. "It was so chaotic. I don't remember seeing anyone in particular, just a wash of faces. People were yelling and shoving each other aside as they tried to get down the ladder. I tried to find you, but there were too many people crowded inside. And then I heard the screams coming from the lawn."

Lana nodded, contemplating her mother's words and Hadley's photos. Eleven seconds seemed quite brief, but it was definitely enough time to cross the short distance from the railing to the ladder. But would the police come to the same conclusion, or only see Gillian's moving towards Priscilla, seconds before she fell?

"Okay, I'm pretty sure Hadley won't do anything with the pictures, like post them online. She wants money, and if she does that, she won't get a penny. Let's both pretend we don't know about the photos and hope she lets it go. Though I do expect her to try to extort money from you tomorrow."

Lana paused a moment to consider the next day's scheduled events. "Tomorrow we are going on a day tour to Alkmaar. It might be better if you don't join us. If you can avoid Hadley, she might give up."

Gillian bobbed her head. "I think you're right. That should give her time to understand I'm not going to pay. I appreciate you letting me know and trusting me enough to ask." Her mother smiled gently as she took Lana's hand, adding, "This is not the Mother's Day trip I had imagined it would be."

Lana squeezed her hand back, then rose, still uncomfortable around her mother. Until she talked to Gillian's assistant, she couldn't trust anything her mother said. "I should go. Tomorrow's going to be a long day, and it's really late. Why don't we talk again after I get back from the tour?"

"I would love that."

Lana half expected her mother to hug her when she left. Gillian waved instead, before gently closing her door.

30

Conclusive Proof

May 7—Day Six of the Wanderlust Tour in Amsterdam

"Lana, help me!" Gillian screamed as two police officers pulled her towards their patrol car.

Lana's group had just returned from a delightful tour of Alkmaar's Cheese Market and was crossing the street towards the hotel when she heard the screams. She sprinted to her mother, reaching the car just as the police were getting Gillian into the backseat.

"What's going on?" she yelled, searching for the lead officer.

The investigator from Zaanse Schans approached her, slapping the roof of the car as he walked past. Its driver sped off before Lana could jump in front of the vehicle.

"We are taking your mother in for questioning. Unfortunately, she didn't wish to join us voluntarily, so we had to resort to more drastic measures."

"What?" *Why did Gillian resist arrest?* Lana wondered. "Priscilla was hit by the blade of a windmill—you said that yourself. It was an accident. So why are you taking my mother in?"

The inspector leaned in so close to Lana that she could smell his musty aftershave. "Because we are no longer certain Priscilla's death was an accident."

Lana's eyes widened as her mind raced. "That doesn't make any sense.

Your forensics team said –"

"We have already run background checks on all of your guests, and I know you used to work as a journalist. That doesn't make you privy to more information, even if it is your mother."

The inspector's emphasis on the phrase "used to be" angered Lana to the core. Suddenly a spark ignited deep inside. Her career had been taken away from her and her reputation tarnished, but recent circumstances dictated that she would soon be welcome back into the fold.

"As a matter of fact, I am still writing freelance articles for several American newspapers. And I bet they would love a sensational exposé about the Dutch police's mistreatment of an American tourist being held in their custody."

The inspector laughed. "You have got to be kidding me. What do you want?"

"To know why you are taking Gillian in for questioning."

He examined her closely, his eyes calculating how much he would have to tell her in order to get her off his back. "The railing around the windmill's observation platform is quite high, and under normal circumstances, a person can't easily fall over. Even if they were hit by the windmill's blades while standing next to the railing, their body would have stayed on the platform and not fallen onto the lawn. It looks like someone pushed Priscilla over the railing as the blade hit her."

"But you don't know for certain that my mother did the pushing," Lana hounded.

"We do have a series of photographs that show your mother standing right next to Priscilla mere seconds before she fell."

Hadley! Lana fumed internally. "That's not conclusive proof –"

"No, it is not, which is why we wish to formally interview Gillian. Her resistance this morning is not encouraging."

Lana sucked in her breath. Gillian's pride being what it was, Lana shouldn't have been surprised by her mother's opposition to being taken in for questioning, especially if it was based on Hadley's photos.

What is that silly girl playing at? Lana smoldered, as the inspector bade her farewell and drove off. When Tammy had called her room this morning and told her that she and Hadley were feeling poorly and would not be joining the tour, Lana had jumped for joy. The last thing she needed was for Hadley to spend the day dropping innuendos about Gillian and the photos. Now she realized that mother and daughter had stayed behind so they could call the police and set up Gillian.

Lana rushed past her group, gathered around Randy in the lobby, and up the stairs to Hadley's room. Her client refused to open the door, despite Lana's pounding.

"How could you share those photos with the police?" Lana yelled through the door instead.

"Mom thought there might be a reward," Hadley responded. She sounded miserable. "But there wasn't."

"You threw my mother to the wolves because you hoped to get rich?" First the whistleblower, and now Hadley. What was wrong with the world? Why did dreams of big payoffs make sane people act so stupidly?

As mad as she was at her mom for helping McGruffin Wood, this was not the karmic payback Lana had been expecting. She turned on her heel and charged down the hallway. When Lana reached the end of it, she realized that she had no idea where she was headed. She took a long, cleansing breath, letting her eyes flutter shut as she considered her options. When she opened them, she knew exactly what she needed to do.

31

Checking the Facts

"Hi, Carly, how are you doing this morning?" Lana asked.

Carly had been Gillian's personal assistant for twenty years, ever since her mother had taken over the reins of Hansen Advertising Agency. The plump, motherly woman had always been kind to her and had done her best to help patch things up with Gillian after Lana's firing. Unfortunately, even her gentle nagging wasn't enough to get Gillian to pick up the phone and actually call her daughter. Or so Lana always thought. Now she knew the truth, that Gillian couldn't face her after her company helped save McGruffin's reputation.

Just how much about the deal and Gillian's involvement did Carly know? Lana's decision on whether to help her mother hinged on Gillian's level of participation in the project and advertising campaign. Lana dreaded making this call, fearing Carly would confirm that Gillian was directly responsible for McGruffin's marketing.

After Lana explained the reason for her call, the line was so quiet she was afraid Carly had hung up. Maybe the assistant didn't recall the McGruffin campaign, after all. "Are you still there?"

"Oh, Lana, I knew you'd find out one day and told Gillian as much. It would have been better for you to have heard it from her, and not how you did."

Hearing Carly confirm both Gillian's secrecy and her agency's involvement brought a tear to her eye. "Do you know if Gillian was leading the project? Can you look that up?" Lana asked, pushing down the anger rising up inside of her.

"I don't have to. That cursed campaign has been on my mind for ten years. We never should have taken it on, if only for moral reasons. Your articles clearly showed how McGruffin was polluting the environment."

Hearing Carly's praise didn't take away the sting of betrayal. "So why did you?"

"I'm a glorified secretary; no one really cares what I think. But I do recall the sales team celebrating signing McGruffin with champagne. It was a big account and quite a coup at the time."

"But was Gillian involved in landing the project?"

"I am positive she was not. Gillian was out of town so much those days, flying around the country helping to get the other affiliates open. I can take a look at her agenda, but I am certain she wasn't even in Seattle when they signed McGruffin."

"Great, could you check her agenda for me right now?"

Carly's displeasure coursed through the international line. "You really don't trust Gillian, do you?"

"No," Lana whispered. "I don't."

Carly huffed. "You are just as stubborn as she is."

The ticking of Carly's fingers flying over the keyboard filled Lana's ear. Moments later she came back on the line. "The Seattle office signed McGruffin on October 7 when Gillian was in New York. The first review session with their clients was two weeks later. Gillian flew from New York to Atlanta that week. She returned to Seattle on November 7 and attended the second review session on November 8. That was when she found out about the McGruffin project."

"But why didn't she cancel it when she discovered her team was helping my enemy?"

Carly ticked her tongue against her teeth. "Lana, be reasonable. Gillian didn't have a choice. She had just spent weeks persuading several East Coast clients to sign with her agency's new offices. If we had dropped the

McGruffin project at that stage, not only would we have wasted hundreds of hours, but I bet those new clients would have looked elsewhere. Once word got out that we cut a campaign at such a late stage, we would have had trouble signing any major clients. Reliability is an important element of our business."

It was Lana's turn to be still and consider Carly's words.

"I know it's not what you wanted to hear, Lana, but it's the truth. Gillian really didn't have a choice. She did ensure that the campaign was a one-time project. Usually when we take on such a large client, we handle all of their marketing for two to three years, before they move on to another agency."

"Do you know if Gillian personally worked on any aspect of the McGruffin Wood campaign?"

"She couldn't have; she didn't even find out about it until the second review session. At that stage, they would have been hammering out the details, not the general marketing concept or visuals. That would have been decided upon in the first session."

"So she wouldn't have had much interaction with anyone working for McGruffin."

"I should think not. She would have introduced herself at the meeting, but in general, she just listens. Her team is more in tune with her client's wishes than she is. Her attendance is all about perception. The clients like knowing the owner is in the room because it makes them feel special, but her team does the work."

"That's good to know." Lana was relieved to know that her mother wasn't actively involved in helping McGruffin thrive and survive. And as much as she didn't like hearing it, Lana understood that her mother would have committed career suicide if she had canceled the McGruffin campaign. There was only one more thing to check.

"Could I ask one more favor? Do you still have access to the meeting notes from the review sessions? The tourist who was killed was a former CEO of McGruffin Wood. Her name was Erin Priscilla Andersen. I would like to know if she attended any of the review sessions."

"Sure, let me take a look." Lana could hear Carly humming softly as she typed. "Here they are. I don't see her name or anyone with the title CEO on the list of attendees at the first or second meeting. McGruffin's vice president of marketing was present at both sessions, but it was a man. Wait, there is a notation about a third and final review session, because they weren't entirely happy with the visuals."

Lana could hear Carly breathing into the phone as she read the documents on her screen. "Yes, it appears E.P. Andersen was present for the final review session. From what I see here, she was the one who didn't approve of the color scheme, but your mother talked her into leaving it as it was. And that's it. It was a short meeting, more of a hand-holding session really."

"Okay, Carly, thanks for checking for me." So that explained why Priscilla recognized and remembered Gillian. But it didn't sound like there were any altercations or arguments. Thus, Gillian had no reason to want to harm Priscilla.

Feeling slightly better, Lana decided to ask Carly one more question. "Hey, since I have you, what do you know about Barry?"

"He's a great guy and really patient with your mom. He's encouraging her to live life, instead of focusing solely on work. She sure needs it. Gillian's not getting any younger, and she's going to have to make a decision about retirement and her successor soon."

Lana was stunned to hear Gillian was considering retirement. Work had been all her mother was interested in—well, since her father died anyway. Lana couldn't envision Gillian anywhere but behind a desk or in a boardroom. "I'm glad to hear that Barry is good for her."

"He really is. You should meet him, after you get back from Seattle. I know he's been trying to meet you for months."

"I'll have to set up an appointment with Mom," Lana said automatically, realizing that if she didn't figure out who did push Priscilla and why, she would probably be meeting Barry in a courthouse.

"Do you think the police will believe Gillian, that she had nothing to do with this?" Carly asked, the concern in her voice evident.

"I hope so. I mean, it doesn't sound like Mom had any reason to harm her," Lana responded, her mind already turning over the next question. If Gillian hadn't pushed Priscilla, who had?

32

Making a To-Do List

"What am I going to do, Dotty?" Lana asked. She had cornered her boss in the hallway, too keyed up to wait until Dotty had returned to her room.

"It sounds like Gillian was being stubborn when the inspector came to talk to her, which wasn't very smart. The police might hold her a little longer as payback. The more important question right now is, who did push Priscilla and how are you going to figure it out?"

"That is the million-dollar question."

"We can't just leave the police to deal with it. You know as well as I do that Priscilla and Gillian are nothing more than two tourists to them. They won't be able to find out more about the possible motives all the way over here in Holland. And unless one of us can prove to the Dutch police that another guest wanted Priscilla gone, they aren't going to take a good look at any of them."

Lana was with the group night and day. If any of them had bumped Priscilla off, she would have a better chance of finding that out than the local police would. And right now, the inspector didn't seem to consider any of the other guests as potential suspects.

Dotty mistook Lana's hesitation as disapproval. "If you don't try to help your mom, you will regret it for the rest of your life."

Lana nodded. "You're right. The way I see it, if someone did intentionally push Priscilla into that windmill's blade, it must have been one of the guests who was on the balcony."

"It's too bad Frieda and Sara were down on the lawn and couldn't see who was up on the observation deck when she fell."

"And I was already down on the second floor. It was so chaotic, but I do recall seeing Anne, Tammy, Paige, Gillian, and Daphne all up there with me. At least they were before Priscilla and I got into that argument."

"Well, it must be one of them," Dotty said resolutely as if this was all settled. "Now all you have to do is figure out which one is a murderer."

* * *

Lana turned on her laptop as soon as she returned to her room. She pulled out a notepad and pen, writing "TO DO" across the top. Underneath it, she wrote out her list of suspects. So far, several of their guests had a reason for despising Priscilla, but who really hated her enough to want her dead?

One glance at the clock told Lana she would only have time to run a basic search before she had to go to bed. Lana couldn't bear leaving Randy to deal with their guests alone, and Dotty was still not feeling completely up to snuff. She had little choice but to help Gillian during her free time.

Lana chose Anne as her first subject. A short article in a local newspaper seven months earlier announced that another cleaning company had won the McGruffin contract. Lana was about to move on when a link to a more recent article caught her eye. An environmental magazine had run a feature on Anne's company and its new commitment to using bio-friendly cleaning products. Since going green, it had signed several new clients, enough that it had hired new employees to fulfill its contracts.

Lana couldn't believe what she was reading. She surfed to Anne's company's website. On the front page was a link to an application form and an announcement stating it was hiring ten full-time employees, to begin as soon as possible.

What the heck was going on? Sara was convinced everything was going

154

wrong in Anne's life, which was why her daughter had moved back home. Yet from what Lana could see, Anne's company was experiencing a huge uptick in business.

Lana tapped her pen against her chin, wondering why Anne would be lying. She already found it suspicious enough that the woman acted so sullen and uninterested when her mother was around, yet went clubbing after Sara went to bed. She was clearly hiding something. But what?

Lana made a note to ask Sara more about why Anne had moved back in and to find out whether she had checked Anne's website lately. That second task would require a delicate touch. As much as Lana liked Sara and felt protective towards her, Anne was her daughter. And she was obviously lying to her mother. Until Lana knew why, she didn't want to be the one to tell Sara the truth.

Daphne had mentioned that, as her mother's personal assistant, she had access to all of Priscilla's files. If Anne did send threatening letters to McGruffin, they might help explain what she was hiding and why. Lana added "Daphne and death threats" to her list of action items.

She moved on to Tammy. One look at her Facebook account confirmed that the older woman was obsessed with getting her thirty-year bonus. Since being made redundant seven months earlier, she had frequently posted articles about McGruffin Wood's profits and tagged her old boss in all of them. *No wonder he responded so quickly to her calls, Tammy was constantly on his case*, Lana thought.

According to her social media posts, Priscilla was the source of all of Tammy's woes, and her old boss was her knight in shining armor being thwarted by the former CEO's greediness. Lana wouldn't be surprised if Tammy had also sent threatening emails to Priscilla. She would have to ask Daphne.

Lana typed Paige's name in next, expecting to see a link to her employer, Zeus Publishing. Yet her name brought up no results. And Lana couldn't find any reference to Paige's name on the company's website or organizational structure. *That's odd*, Lana thought, while scanning the short list of writers on its staff. Though she doubted that Paige had anything to do with Priscilla's death, Lana dutifully added the writer's name to her list. She would have to ask Daphne whether she had a business card or contact information for Paige. And Lana would love to speak with one of her fellow writers and ask about her unorthodox approach. Her obsession with Priscilla's childhood was rather strange for a biographer, especially considering it was Priscilla's leadership skills that made her life book-worthy.

Gillian was next. Based on her conversation with Carly, Lana could confidently scratch her mother off of her list of suspects.

Last up was Daphne. One yawn turned into three. Lana looked longingly at her bed, before her curiosity about the recently orphaned woman invigorated her enough to type her name into the search engine. The numerous results were as powerful as a jolt of caffeine.

However, almost all of the articles were about Priscilla and only mentioned that Daphne was her assistant. A few were features in architectural and home decorating magazines. A long article in *Architectural Digest* featured images taken in each of Priscilla's five homes. From the looks of it, she'd had expensive taste in furnishings and had preferred to live in secluded mansions close to America's most famous beaches.

Lana had not considered how wealthy Priscilla might be. Apparently being CEO paid well. Suddenly Priscilla's threats about disinheriting Daphne if she didn't do what her mother wanted took on new meaning. The dead woman was worth a fortune, and Lana had to assume that everything would go to her only living relative: her daughter, Daphne.

As she stared at the screen, her eyes began drooping shut. Lana turned off her laptop and crawled into bed, telling herself she would get up early and continue her investigation in the morning.

33

Agatha Christie on the Rocks

Lana brushed the charcoal stick lightly over the thick paper, hoping she was pushing down hard enough this time to create the effect their teacher desired.

The workshop leader watched her carefully, examining the result as soon as Lana put the charcoal down. "Much better. You see how, when applied lightly, the charcoal allows the paper to come through, creating a more realistic shadow."

"Yes, I do," Lana said, marveling at how each medium created a different effect on the canvas or paper. Her group was in the Rijksmuseum's Drawing School and was almost finished with an hour-long introduction to artistic mediums. It was fun to try drawing with ink, charcoal, pencils, felt pens, and watercolor paints, but Lana quickly discovered that she had no talent for it.

Looking around at her clients' canvases, she realized several of them did. Frieda and Franny had created detailed and realistic portraits of each other. Franny was not only beautiful, but also artistically talented. If the woman wasn't so nice, Lana might have been tempted to throttle her.

Randy, Sara, and Anne had produced decent landscapes, but nothing to write home about. Dotty and Sally had chosen to draw dogs with sweaters on, a familiar topic for both of them. The results were as adorable as their knitted creations. Tammy and Hadley couldn't be bothered to follow along with the lesson, each more interested in their smartphones than putting pen to paper.

Since Priscilla's death, Tammy's phone hadn't left her hand. She was in constant contact with her old boss, who was convinced Tammy had a fighting shot at receiving her bonus after all. At least, that's what Tammy gladly told anyone who would listen. Lana was amazed at how quickly Tammy was getting her way, now that Priscilla was gone.

Lana had not been looking forward to the tour of the Rijksmuseum this morning, but it ended up being the perfect distraction from her current troubles. However, by the time they were finished with the drawing lesson, dark thoughts had taken over again, leaving her feeling restless and distracted.

She followed her group in a daze as they traversed the cobblestoned streets of Amsterdam. Bikes, pedestrians, delivery trucks, and cars all fought for space on the narrow strips of road running parallel to the many canals crisscrossing the city. After almost getting run over by an angry bicyclist, Lana pushed her thoughts aside and focused on getting herself and her group to Pulitzer's Bar in one piece.

Randy led them to the upscale bar on the Keizergracht. The elegant space was divided into several small rooms, almost like a home, and each was decorated as if the owner had just stepped out. The art deco furnishings and fixtures made it a timeless and relaxing space.

Her group settled around several small tables in what could have once been the living room. Luckily most were getting along well enough that all she and Randy had to do was take their orders, then sit back and relax. Lana was grateful; her mind was racing through her list of suspects on an unending loop that she couldn't switch off.

She chuckled when she saw the bar's cocktail menu was inspired by characters in Agatha Christie's *Murder on the Orient Express*. Each of the twelve suspects in her mystery had a drink dedicated to them. Lana waffled between "The Gangster" or "The Conductor," ultimately settling for "The Maid" when she noticed lemon sherbet was one of the ingredients.

The drink list made Lana think of her own group—the cleaner, retiree, personal assistant, social influencer, writer, and advertising executive. What would her suspects' drinks be made of?

More importantly, who were her prime suspects, and why would they have wanted to harm Priscilla? She ticked them off in her mind: Anne for revenge. Tammy for money. Daphne for freedom.

Chances were high that it was Tammy or Daphne. Lana didn't think Anne had the backbone. But her sneaking around was strange, as were the news articles on her website about hiring more employees. Why was Anne lying to her mom about her company's success—or lack thereof?

Since Priscilla's death, Tammy had become quite full of confidence. What had changed? Her crusade to get her long-coveted bonus was coming to fruition. But did Tammy come on this tour in order to harm Priscilla? Or had she made a spur-of-the-moment decision to use the chaos and confusion up on that windmill to her advantage?

Her bonus was equivalent to a year's salary, which Tammy made clear was a substantial amount. And Tammy was so dedicated to her daughter that she might have done so, in order to help Hadley get her business off the ground.

After months of leading a campaign to have all of the laid-off employees reimbursed, it would have been tempting for her to get rid of the only remaining obstacle standing in her way. And both Hadley and Tammy had repeatedly shown that they were heartless and extraordinarily self-centered. Lana wondered whether Tammy could have pushed Priscilla off the railing and suffered no remorse. *Yes* resonated in her mind.

Yet, any way she looked at it, it seemed that Daphne would benefit the most from her mother's untimely death. With Priscilla gone, Daphne was instantly rich and free to be with the man of her dreams. Many had killed for less. But why now? Was it because of her boyfriend? They did seem quite serious. Or was it this adopted child Paige kept harping on?

Had Priscilla given a child up for adoption, and did Daphne know about it? Would Daphne have killed her mother in order to prevent the truth from coming out, so she could inherit everything? To Lana, Daphne didn't seem like the murdering type.

Unsure how to proceed, Lana tried a different tactic, asking herself, *Did all three women have the opportunity to push Priscilla?*

Lana wished that she could answer her own question. As soon as her hands had wrapped around Priscilla's neck, her mind had gone blank. And so far, nothing was coming back. It was as if her brain had wiped the event away. She recalled the chaos that her primal screams had caused, people running every which way after mistaking her for a terrorist, a shooter, or a bomber. All she knew for certain was that the three had been out on the observation deck before Paige told Lana about Priscilla paying off the whistleblower. Any of them could have given Priscilla enough of a push to send her over the edge and into the turning blade of that blasted windmill, if they stuck around after she and Priscilla began to fight.

Randy put a hand on her shoulder, breaking her train of thought. When she looked up at him, he seemed concerned. "Everything alright?"

"Yes, sorry, my mind was drifting."

"You look so distraught. I hope you weren't thinking badly about Alex," he teased.

Lana blushed. "Certainly not. You were right; your brother is pretty wonderful."

"He thinks the same about you. He won't stop messaging me with questions about you. I've never seen him so smitten before." Lana's smile made Randy chuckle. "I'm glad to see he's not wasting his time." He gestured to their group. "Should we see if our guests want another round?"

"Yes, that's a great idea." Lana rose and walked over to the Fantastic Four. As she approached, she heard Franny say to Anne, "Nice moves last night. What was the name of the club I saw you in? I want to tell a girlfriend about it. Was it Jimmy Woo's or Escape?"

"Oh, you must be mistaken, I wasn't out clubbing last night," Anne stammered.

When Lana looked over at Anne, she was shooting furtive glances at her mother, Sara.

Sara chuckled, apparently unaware of her daughter's distress. "Anne never goes out anymore. I would be thrilled if she did," Sara muttered to Frieda loudly enough for them all to hear.

Evidently flustered, Franny turned to her mother and let the conversation drop. Anne blushed before running off to the bathroom.

What is Anne playing at? It must have been Anne in the hallway, all dressed up to go clubbing. But why would she keep denying it so vehemently? Anne's actions, on top of her lying about her business's failures, put her back onto Lana's suspect list.

"Say, Sara, when did Anne move back home?" she asked.

"Oh, gosh, about six months ago. Soon after she lost that McGruffin contract, she found out her boyfriend was cheating on her. It was a rough time. Since they were living together, it made sense for her to move back home, until she could find a new place. And since my husband passed, it has been pretty lonely living alone. It was nice to dote on someone again." Sara stopped and gazed out the window, apparently lost in her thoughts.

Her use of the past tense wasn't lost on Lana. "And are you still happy with her being home?"

"Now I just want her to get off her backside. A mopey housemate isn't exactly stimulating company. But until her business gets back on its feet, I can't in good conscience ask her to move out."

"At least you get to see your daughter on a regular basis," Frieda said. "Mine can't be bothered to fly home these days."

Franny rolled her eyes. "Mom, it's my job that takes me around the world. It's not like I'm trying to get away from you. Once things calm down, I'll be back in Seattle so much you'll probably get sick of me."

"And when is that going to happen? I'm not going to live forever, you know," Frieda huffed.

"I figure I have another two years before I'm too old for the top contracts. That gives me time to decide on my next career move. I'm still considering a number of different business ideas."

"Where are you going to get the startup capital? Getting a business off the ground costs money. And all of your gallivanting around the world can't be cheap."

"My work pays for the planes, hotels, and food, on top of my salary. And trust me, I'm paid well for the work I do. Most of what I earn, I invest, just like you and Dad taught me. After I retire from modeling, I should be able to do whatever I want."

Frieda shone with pride. "I knew I raised you right."

"I have another surprise for you," Franny said. "I'm going to be partnering with a modeling school back in Seattle. If things work out the way I hope, I'll be back home every three months to lead a week-long workshop."

Frieda's shrieks of delight startled most of the bar's customers. She pulled her daughter into a bear hug. "That's what I wanted to hear most of all."

Sara stood up, apparently only now aware that her own daughter was still AWOL. "I better go see where Anne's gotten off to."

"Why don't I go? You enjoy your drink," Lana said. It was time to find out what exactly Anne was hiding and why.

She found Anne outside the bar, standing by the service entrance, smoking a cigarette. When she saw Lana approach, she dropped the butt and took a step away.

"Hi, Anne."

"Oh, hi, Lana. I was looking for the toilet, but I must have gone through the wrong door," she said nervously.

"I can smell the smoke on your sweater," Lana said.

Anne looked at her clothes, stricken.

"Listen, can I be blunt? I saw on your company website that you've already secured new contracts and are hiring more employees. So why are you pretending to be down in the dumps and telling everyone that your company is on the verge of bankruptcy?"

"What? You must be mistaken," Anne said as she tried to walk around Lana.

Lana grabbed her client's arm. "Will you stop with the 'poor me' charade? I saw you sneaking out of the hotel all dolled up. If you don't come clean with me, I am going to tell the police about you lying and acting so strange. My mother didn't hurt Priscilla. I don't know if you did, but if bringing you to the police's attention gets them to let her go, then I will do it."

"No! It's not like that," Anne said and leaned heavily against the wall. "After we lost the McGruffin contract and my boyfriend dumped me, I was having trouble getting out of bed in the morning. Mom really helped me get through a tough couple of months. And it was so nice to have someone else cook and clean for me, for a change. After I started landing more clients and things began picking up at work, I just couldn't face being on my own again and having to do everything myself again. I do most of my work online so Mom didn't notice that I was working again. She thought I was just watching television and surfing the internet."

Lana couldn't believe what she was hearing. "So you've been pretending to be helpless so your mom will take care of you?"

"Pretty much," Anne said, hanging her head.

"Geez, how old are you?"

"Look, I'm not exactly proud of my actions, but it is what it is. You aren't going to tell my mom, are you?"

Lana looked long and hard at Anne. As much as she wanted to say something, she knew that Anne needed to tell Sara herself. "Only if you promise to tell her before this trip is over."

Anne nodded vigorously. "Yes, okay, give me a chance to figure out how, and I will."

"Just tell her the truth. It's easiest that way. We better go inside; she's looking for you."

When they returned, Daphne was throwing her napkin onto the ground and storming out of the room. Lana went over to Randy and whispered, "What was that all about?"

"Daphne and Paige were at it again. Whatever it is that Paige keeps asking about, Daphne does not want to discuss it with her."

"I'll try to keep Paige distracted, or at least away from Daphne. It isn't really helping the group spirit having her storm off like this."

"I don't know; between you and Priscilla fighting, and now Paige and Daphne, the older ladies have plenty to gossip about," he said with a smile. "And they don't seem to be bothered by Priscilla's death. If anything, Tammy has been in a much better mood since the accident."

Lana rested her hand on his arm. "Thanks for saying accident."

"I don't believe your mother hurt Priscilla, and neither do Dotty or Sally. Whatever you need to do to help clear her name, you go ahead and do it.

Dotty's ready to step in and help, if need be."

"That's really kind of you both; thanks, Randy. Right now, all I can do is wait for Jeremy to get back to me, hopefully with new information that can help us determine who would have wanted Priscilla dead."

"There doesn't seem to be a shortage," Randy said.

"I'm afraid you're right. Though we can scratch one name off of the list. I talked to Gillian's assistant and know for certain that my mom didn't have anything to do with the McGruffin account. And she met Priscilla only briefly during one of the review sessions, but there was no argument or disagreement recorded in the notes. Gillian has no reason to want to harm Priscilla. It doesn't help prove her innocence to the police, but it is a relief," Lana admitted.

"I can imagine." Randy's phone began beeping softly. "Gosh, I'm sorry, Lana. We have to get our group to the Begijnhof for our next tour."

"Sure, no problem."

"Are you certain that you're up for this?"

"Absolutely," Lana said, turning her smile up. "I've been looking forward to seeing it."

While she was looking forward to the tour, it wasn't the architecture or churches that interested her right now—it was her guests. She would have to observe them carefully and see whether any of her suspects slipped up. Considering the evidence, Daphne was still Lana's prime suspect. She would have to stay close to her and hope that the orphan slipped up.

"I'll go find Daphne, then we can head out," Randy said.

34

Who Gains the Most?

"How are you doing, Daphne?" Lana asked as casually as she could. After they returned from their long day of tours, Daphne had headed straight for the hotel bar. Before her stood the largest margarita Lana had ever seen. And the glass was almost empty.

Their tour of the Begijnhof gardens and churches was quite short, and she hadn't had a chance to chat with Daphne during it. As much as she was convinced either Tammy, Anne, or Daphne had pushed Priscilla off the windmill, she was also becoming convinced it had been a spur-of-the-moment decision. No one could have known that she and Priscilla would get into a fight out on the windmill's observation platform.

Whoever did it must have seen their chance and grabbed it, before they could really think it through. Did they feel guilty about their actions? If that was the case, then none of her guests were cold-blooded killers. No one on this tour was showing remorse; in fact everyone seemed happy to have Priscilla gone.

Daphne had the most to gain and she didn't seem upset about her mother's death in the slightest. That bothered Lana, but it didn't convince her of Daphne's guilt. If she had seized the opportunity and pushed her mom over the railing, why wasn't she pretending to be distraught or miss Priscilla? It seemed to Lana a better reaction than scheduling a vacation with her boyfriend twenty-four hours after her mother died.

Yet the information Paige shared with Lana was quite convincing. Daphne had been trapped in a job she hated, working for and living with a woman she despised, and couldn't continue dating the man she loved without risking being disinherited. Now that Priscilla was gone, she would get the man, houses, and money. From what Lana found out online about Priscilla's properties and investments, she assumed Daphne wouldn't have to worry about working for the rest of her life.

"Never been better! If only I could get Paige to leave the tour, my life would be perfect." Based on how badly Daphne slurred her words, the alcohol was already having an effect on her.

As much as Lana hated taking advantage of her guest's inebriated state, this was the perfect moment to try to extract more information out of her, she realized.

Lana sat on the barstool next to her, waving the barman away when he asked what she wanted to drink. "What do you mean, Daphne? Is Paige bothering you? I did see you two fighting at Pulitzer's Bar."

Daphne shook her head. "That girl has crazy ideas in her head. Do you know Paige is convinced that Mom gave a child up for adoption twenty-seven years ago? Paige isn't interested in Mom's career at all. All she cares about is her childhood and this mystery baby. Even if I wanted to, I can't help her. Mom had a falling-out with her parents before I was born, and I've never even met them. She flat-out refused to tell me anything about her life before thirty. But I can't believe she had a child before then; she had always said I was the daughter she could never have."

"Wait—are you adopted, too?"

"Yes, I am. My parents died in a car crash when I was two. Priscilla was good friends with both of them, and after they passed, she adopted me. Is Paige leaving the tour? I sure hope she does."

"As far as I know, she is staying. And I can't really force her to leave the hotel."

"That's too bad. I already asked the police if I could fly back to the States, but they need me to stick around a few more days to deal with getting Mom home. I hope they hurry up and release her; I'm flying to Miami after this to

166

meet up with my boyfriend. Now that Mom's gone, we don't have to sneak around anymore."

"Oh, that sounds like fun," Lana said as neutrally as possible, knowing it was expected of her. Annoyance about being inconvenienced by her mother's corpse was not at all the reaction Lana had been expecting.

Lana started to rise, when another thought struck her. "Daphne, who did you say Paige was working for?"

"Zeus Publishing; they have offices in New York and San Francisco. I can get you her business card, if you want; I found it in Priscilla's hotel room."

"That would be great; thanks, Daphne." Lana hesitated before adding, "How did the publishers contact Priscilla? By phone or email?"

Daphne thought a moment. "Mom received an email from the president of Zeus Publishing telling her about their idea of including her in a series of biographies they were planning on publishing later this year. I can't remember his name, but he did ask if she was interested and available. I answered most of her correspondence, but in this case she replied to him directly, saying that she was. Soon after the president sent her an email introducing Paige as one of their in-house writers and letting her know to expect a call from her. I believe she did call Mom later that afternoon. The next thing I knew, Mom was adding Paige to this tour."

Daphne took a sip of her margarita, thinking back to the chain of events. "Mom asked me to send Paige the airline tickets and hotel reservations. She did stop by our house and conduct a preliminary interview with Mom a few days later, but we were leaving for Amsterdam in a week, so Mom asked if they could wait and do most of the work during this holiday."

The younger woman chuckled. "Mom always did prefer work above pleasure. No, that's not fair. To Mom, work was pleasure. She loved being in charge." Daphne took another gulp of her margarita, then hiccupped as she lowered the glass.

Lana felt sorry for Daphne. She could tell from Daphne's cynical tone that she and her mother hadn't had a very good relationship. Lana knew firsthand how painful that could be. Regardless, she was here to help set her own mother free. Lana pushed on with her questions.

"I don't mean to pry, but who could have benefited from Priscilla's death?"

Daphne stared at Lana as if she was crazy. "All of humanity. She was quite a horror, when I think about it. Just for the record—I didn't know about McGruffin dumping chemicals, nor did I know about her helping to destroy your career. I'm sorry for you."

"Thanks," Lana whispered. Daphne's candidness dared her to ask a personal question. "Why did you let her control your life?"

Daphne snorted. "I felt like I didn't have much choice. She'd sabotaged my career and threatened to disinherit me if I didn't marry her stockbroker's son. Do you know how great it feels to finally be free to live my own life? Mom has been treating me like a ten-year-old for years. She refused to acknowledge that I am a capable person. Do you know I was on track to being the youngest vice president in the company when she made me her personal assistant?" Daphne spat the words out. "I took a demotion to help her out on the condition that when she retired, I would be able to step back into marketing as a vice president. But when she retired, she took me with her and appointed a man to the job that she'd promised me. So much for girl power."

Daphne downed the rest of her drink, then signaled for another. "She ruined my chances at a career, just as she ruined every relationship I've had. Your mom did me a favor. Cheers to Gillian." Daphne burped out a laugh.

"My mom didn't kill Priscilla, Daphne."

"The Dutch police certainly think so. Cheers to Hadley for being a social media nut." Daphne raised her empty glass in a salute.

As angry as her words made her feel, Lana couldn't help but feel bad for Daphne. All those mind games and power trips she had suffered under. At least Gillian had let her be, instead of trying to control Lana's life.

"I know the police have my mother in custody, but I do not believe she pushed Priscilla, at least not on purpose. But I don't know who else would have. You mentioned that you had access to Priscilla's emails and paperwork. Could you check and see if you can find the threatening letters Anne and Tammy sent to McGruffin Wood? They may be important enough to show to the Dutch police. They are the only two guests who had a motive to harm

Priscilla," Lana fibbed to her prime suspect.

"Sure, I can do that. I do recall that Tammy's letters were quite disturbing. Not only did she send several death threats, but she also tried to sneak into Mom's office on her last day. Lord knows what Tammy was planning on doing. I had to have security remove her. Then Anne—the cleaner—tried to start a lawsuit, but it never got off the ground because it was clear McGruffin owed her nothing. She and some of her crew protested outside of our offices for days, until the police finally made them leave."

"This is great information, Daphne." Lana smiled encouragingly. "The police really need to know about this, before the tour ends. That way they can question any other suspects while they are still here in Amsterdam."

"Okay. The threatening emails Tammy and Anne sent to Mom should still be on the server. It might take me a while to find them, but if I do, I can print them off for you, so you can give them to the police. I'll have another look through my files and see what I can find on all of the guests on this tour, in case we are missing another connection."

"That would be wonderful. Thank you."

"I can't imagine that any of the other guests did it. But then they have as much reason to harm Mom as Gillian did."

"Actually, Gillian had no reason to harm Priscilla," Lana stated resolutely.

"I don't know. If someone humiliated me like Priscilla did you, my mother would have done everything in her power to destroy that person. Not out of love, mind you. Her personal pride would have demanded it."

Lana shook her head. "We aren't that close. I don't think my mom would risk jail in order to save my honor. But it's a nice thought."

"I don't know. She might think the same thing about you, yet here you are, playing detective."

Lana let the words sink in. Would Gillian try to save her if the situation was reversed? She had to believe her mother would. Regardless of how far they'd grown apart, they were still flesh and blood. Lana couldn't just let her mother rot in jail. She wouldn't be able to live with herself if she didn't try to help Gillian, no matter how hopeless it seemed.

35

Threatening Letters

May 8—Day Seven of the Wanderlust Tour in Amsterdam

"Hey Lana, wait up," Daphne called out as Lana was heading down the hallway to the breakfast hall. After how inebriated Daphne had been last night, Lana figured she would have slept in, or at least stayed in her hotel room to nurse a nasty hangover.

Tammy and Hadley walked past, nodding as they went. It was early, but most of her guests seemed to be up and on their way downstairs, as well.

After a long night of internet searches, Lana hadn't found any new or incriminating information about any of her guests. Unless either Daphne found something useful in her mother's documents, or Jeremy's reporters discovered something in their investigation into McGruffin Wood, Lana feared her investigation had hit a dead end.

Lana doubled back to the younger woman. Lana could hear doors opening and closing up and down the hallway as more guests made their way downstairs. She waved hello to Frieda and Franny as they passed by, keeping her focus on Daphne.

Daphne waited until they were out of sight before saying, "I found the threatening letters that Tammy and Anne sent. I'll check for information on the rest of the guests later and get you anything I find this afternoon. If I can't print them off at reception, I'll email them to you. Is that okay?"

"More than okay. It's wonderful—thank you. And you can skip the paper trail if you want. Email is perfect. Oh, and please don't forget Paige's contact information."

"What about contacting me?" Paige asked as she rounded the corner.

"Oh, I was talking to Daphne about the biography. It's nothing important," Lana stammered.

Paige stopped and examined Lana intently. Lana bounced on her heels, feeling uncomfortable under Paige's gaze. When the writer finally nodded and moseyed on down the hallway, Lana felt a wave of relief. She made a mental note to call the publishing house Paige worked for and try to find out more about both the biography and writer.

"When should I come by and pick them up?" Lana asked after the hallway was again clear of guests.

"I am going to have to skip the morning tour," Daphne said, a sour expression on her face. "The police need me to deal with more paperwork concerning the repatriation of Mom's body."

"I am so sorry. If you would rather search tomorrow, I understand."

"It's fine. The police stuff shouldn't take more than an hour. Looking up the information will give me something to do. Why don't you stop by after lunch, say, one o'clock?"

Despite Daphne's helpfulness, it did seem as if the recently orphaned woman was still the one with the most to gain—both financially and romantically—from Priscilla's death. Perhaps the paperwork Daphne had found about the other guests would change Lana's mind. She was well aware that if Daphne was involved, there was a chance that she would hold back or perhaps even make up information to try to shift suspicion to another. Still, right now Daphne was Lana's only way of accessing Priscilla's paperwork.

Lana smiled as warmly as she could. "Sounds great."

36

Jeremy Gets in Touch

Their morning walking tour of the Waterland region, just north of Amsterdam, was quite lovely. The land was crisscrossed with tiny canals and streams cutting through flat fields and pastures, broken further up by several small villages. The wetlands were filled with migrating birds of all colors and shapes.

The soothing Dutch landscape helped bring peace to her mind. The three villages they visited—Marken, Volendam, and Monnickendam—were all well-preserved examples of the fishing villages that once dominated the South Sea. Beautiful marinas situated in the hearts of the cities were filled with lovely wooden ships. Many were reminiscent of the seventeenth-century schooners the Dutch were known for. The clusters of older ladies wearing traditional dresses, wooden clogs, and lacy caps on their heads helped solidify Lana's feeling that they had literally stepped back in time.

Unfortunately for Lana, her mind was so preoccupied with Jeremy's investigation and what Daphne might find that she had trouble listening to their guide. Did Daphne kill her own mother for the money? All Daphne wanted to do was live her life on her own terms, something Priscilla seemed to have trouble accepting. Now that Priscilla was gone, Daphne didn't have to worry about work, a place to live, or her mother badmouthing her boyfriend. When she considered who might have wanted Priscilla dead, Daphne's name still topped her suspect list.

Her group had just stepped onto the bus to head back to Amsterdam, when Lana's phone rang. She glanced at the incoming number and answered it. "Give me just a second, Jeremy," she said as she waved to Randy, currently at the back of the bus. Lana held up the phone. "I need to take this call, is that alright?"

"Sure," he called out. "Okay, folks, let's take our seats so our driver can get us back to our hotel."

Lana made her way to a seat at the front of the bus, well away from her guests. "Okay, Jeremy, we have a thirty-minute bus ride back to Amsterdam. I am all ears."

"We found him, Lana; we found the whistleblower. And he is prepared to come clean about everything."

"What?" Lana whispered, tears of joy already forming in her eyes. "He didn't even try to deny it?"

"It would have been ridiculous of him to try to do so. We found the money trail and confronted him with it. He's a wreck, Lana. Apparently his wife is the one who encouraged him to contact you and to testify in court. She's an environmental activist and wanted to make McGruffin Wood pay. When she found out he had taken a bribe instead of testifying, she divorced him, moved back to her parents' house, and took their kids with her. Then she sued him for an exorbitant alimony and child support that he can no longer pay. He's living in a run-down trailer park outside of Tacoma and drinks his day away."

"That slimy bastard got what he deserved," Lana said, her voice choked with emotion. It was slightly comforting to know that her source had destroyed his own life, not just her and Jeremy's careers, with his lies.

"Is he willing to go on the record this time and tell the truth about his role in my articles and his deception during the libel lawsuit?"

"He is. Apparently his kids won't speak to him, and that breaks his heart most of all. I believe him, Lana. I really do think he's going to do the right thing this time. For his kids, not for us."

"I'll believe it when I see it in print," Lana said, unable to keep the bitterness out of her voice.

"Lana, do you realize what this will mean? Both of our names will be cleared, and the world will finally know that you did not lie about your sources or the information."

Jeremy's words released a floodgate of tears and emotion. After ten long years of treating her like a pariah, everyone would finally know that she wasn't a liar. Anger, disappointment, and relief all washed over her.

"And from what you've told me so far, an article about Priscilla Andersen's death might be the perfect article to come back with," Jeremy continued.

"What do you mean, come back?"

"Lana, don't you get it? Your name is going to be cleared. There will be no reason for newspapers to shun you. In fact, I bet these articles are going to make you a hot commodity. I wouldn't be surprised if you had several offers to come back to work, once this hits the press."

Lana grew nervous, suddenly unsure whether she was ready to be in the spotlight. "Do you think you could have your team leave me out of the article?"

"No way! You are the story, Lana, whether you like it or not."

Lana sucked up her tears and tried to look at this situation rationally, as Jeremy was. He was right; she was the story, as was her source's deception. Would this article's publication mean she could go work as a journalist again? What if the *Seattle Chronicle* offered her a job? Would her old colleagues welcome her back with open arms? Could she happily work again with the same people who had badmouthed her to anyone who would listen for the past decade?

And if another newspaper offered her a job, would it be out of sensationalism or because they respected her as a journalist? Who was she kidding; her reputation had been in the toilet for ten years. Anyone who wanted her on their team would be doing so with an eye on the publicity her byline could bring them.

"I need some time to process this all, Jeremy."

"Sure, okay. It's a lot to take in. But before you go, how is the investigation into Priscilla's death coming? Is your mother still the prime suspect? There's even more reason now to find out who killed her, don't you think? I sure hope your mom is not involved."

Lana sighed. He was right. If she was offered a reporter's position again, the first question any editor would ask was what ideas she had for new articles. And like it or not, she was part of a doozy of a murder investigation involving two powerful Seattle businesswomen.

"So far, Priscilla's daughter, Daphne, has the strongest motive. Paige, Priscilla's ghostwriter, told me about how Priscilla hated Daphne's boyfriend and had messed up a job opportunity for her. Paige is staying on the tour because she is so certain that Daphne is involved in Priscilla's death and she wants to get the scoop for her biography."

"That's odd. Readers interested in a biography about corporate leaders don't generally appreciate that sort of gossipy conspiracy. Who did you say she was working for again?"

"Zeus Publishing."

"Really? They don't normally publish biographies. I thought crime fiction was their specialty. Now, yeah, that might explain why Paige is so interested in finding out who murdered Priscilla."

Lana could hear a baby crying in the background, its screams rapidly rising in octave.

"Ah, the music of angels. My daughter is awake. I better go get her out of her crib. Good luck with your investigation. I hope you're taking lots of notes."

"Thanks, Jeremy; good luck with yours, too. And give that beautiful baby girl a kiss for me."

37

Screaming Bloody Murder

As soon as her group was back inside the hotel, Lana excused herself and went up to Daphne's room, curious to see whether she had found any more connections between Priscilla and the other guests.

When Lana arrived at her hotel room, Daphne's door was ajar. *That's odd,* she thought. Lana knocked anyway, but there was no response.

"Daphne, are you in there?" Lana listened carefully and realized Daphne's shower was running. *Why did she leave the door open if she's taking a shower?* Lana wondered. Unsure whether she should call the hotel reception first, Lana decided to poke her head inside and call out again, hoping Daphne would be able to hear her above the water that way.

When Lana pushed open the door slightly and popped her head inside, the sight before her made her scream bloody murder.

* * *

A half hour later, Lana sat on the edge of her hotel room bed, shivering slightly as she answered questions from the same detective who was handling Priscilla's suspicious death. Someone had smothered poor Daphne and left her lifeless body behind on the floor of her hotel room. It must have been someone she knew or someone posing as hotel staff, because she'd left the shower on when she went to answer the door.

Was Daphne killed by the same person who'd pushed Priscilla over the windmill's railing? Lana would guess so; the two victims were mother and daughter. Their deaths could have something to do with their family and not necessarily McGruffin Wood.

How Lana wished she had access to Priscilla's documents. Now that Daphne was dead, she wouldn't be able to read the threatening letters from Anne and Tammy, nor check for other guests' connections to Priscilla.

"Why did you enter Daphne's room?" the officer asked.

"She asked me to stop by her room after lunch so she could give me some documents she had found. They were threatening letters two of the guests on my tour had sent to Priscilla, when she was still the CEO of McGruffin Wood."

"May I see them?"

"That's the thing, Daphne hadn't given them to me yet. I went to her room to collect them, but as soon as I saw her body, I ran back to my room and called the police and hotel reception." Lana shivered as she recalled Daphne's lifeless corpse shrouded in a white bathrobe spread out across the hotel room floor like a ball gown.

"Are you certain there was no paperwork left out on her desk or bed?" Lana asked the inspector, unwilling to accept that the documents Daphne had said she had found were missing. Which either meant Daphne hadn't had time to print them off or that she had lied and had not planned to give anything to Lana. A third possibility was that Daphne's killer had taken the documents with them.

"No, we did not find any paperwork in her hotel room."

"Could you check her email and see if she had saved an email to me as a draft?" Lana had already checked her email while waiting for the police to arrive, but she had not received any new messages from Daphne.

"We didn't find a computer in her room."

"She must have had a laptop with her. Daphne has been looking up information for Paige, the woman who is writing a biography about Priscilla.

And she was going to do the same for me, this morning." Lana chewed on her bottom lip, pondering the situation when her mother popped into her brain.

"What is going to happen to my mother? Whoever killed Daphne probably killed Priscilla, and since Mom is in your custody, it couldn't have been her."

"For all we know, there are two killers active. This crime does not yet rule your mother out."

"How can you be so certain?"

"Witness statements and photographic evidence suggests that your mother is lying about her movements right before Priscilla was killed. Yet she remains steadfast in her statement that she was by the ladder when Priscilla fell. Until Gillian tells us the truth or we find new evidence pointing to another killer, we will continue to hold her in our custody."

Lana cursed her mother's stubbornness. Why was she lying? Or was she also suffering from a memory lapse, like Lana was, about those precious seconds before Priscilla fell over the edge?

She shook her head. "I know my mom did not do this, which means it must be someone in my group. What are you going to do about it?"

The inspector sighed heavily. "Short of arresting all of you, there is not much we can do at this point."

"Until another one of us is killed, you mean?"

The officer glared at Lana, before adding, "I will post an officer to stand guard in your hallway and lobby, in the hope that their presence scares off the perpetrator. My team is going to investigate Daphne's murder, and we hope to catch her killer before anyone else is harmed. But your being Americans does make our job more difficult. We are working with the Seattle police, in case there is a local angle to these crimes. My team is currently interviewing all of the guests staying on your floor, most of which are part of your tour group. Other than that, you will have to wait to let my team work."

Lana nodded, unhappy to hear him say this but knowing it was the truth. She thought on her guests, wondering who was coldblooded enough to murder two people and why. Were these premeditated murders or two murders of opportunity? Had Daphne found something in her mother's documents that got her killed? Or had her killer always been planning on ridding the world of both Priscilla and Daphne, before this trip even started?

Lana had been convinced that Daphne did it. She had put up with her mother's humiliation and rejection for so long. She had also been out on the windmill's balcony and could have run back out and pushed Priscilla over, without anyone having noticed her doing so in all that chaos.

Yet now that she was dead, Lana had to find another suspect. Neither Tammy nor Anne had issues with Daphne, so far as Lana knew. But they might have heard Lana and Daphne talking in the hallway, when Daphne promised to search for the death threats Tammy and Anne had sent to Priscilla.

Suddenly Lana remembered that Paige had also been privy to their conversation. She'd even interrupted to ask why Lana wanted her contact information. But as much as Paige gave Lana the creeps, she couldn't think of why the writer would want to harm Priscilla or Daphne, let alone kill them.

Lana thought on the other guests, unable to think of any connection between them and either victim. She bashed her knuckles against her temples. Nothing made sense right now—no one had enough of a motive to harm them both. At least, so far as she knew. Which meant whoever did kill them was heartless, calculating, and a great actress.

Lana was going to have to keep her eyes open and her wits about her if everyone was going to survive the rest of this tour.

38

A Mother's Love

Mother's Day—Day Eight of the Wanderlust Tour in Amsterdam

Lana looked around the hotel lobby, double-checking that all of her guests had arrived. When she realized they were one short, Lana caught Randy's eye and threw her hands up.

"I don't see Paige," Lana said after he crossed over to her.

"Is she planning on coming with us today?"

"I thought she was joining us. Should I go up to her room?"

"That would be great, thanks," Randy said.

Lana was almost to Paige's hotel room door when she heard the writer's voice coming from around the next corner. She was on the phone, from the sound of it, and quite excited. Lana stood still so as to better eavesdrop.

"You need to file the claim now, not after I get back," Paige insisted, then grew quiet in order to, Lana assumed, listen to the response.

"I don't care if she's not even in the ground yet. It's better to do it now, before others jump in line. Who knows what she promised to people."

Too late, Lana grasped that Paige was rapidly approaching. Before she could find a place to hide, Paige rounded the corner. Her eyes widened when she noticed Lana.

"Hi, I was just on my way to your room. We are about to leave and weren't certain if you were planning on joining us today," Lana said.

"You better believe I'm coming," Paige responded while shoving her phone into her pocket, acting as if nothing out of the ordinary had just happened.

"So how is your biography going? Will you still be able to accomplish what you set out to do, now that Priscilla and Daphne are gone?"

"Oh, yes, I'm right on track." Paige smiled so serenely, yet the warmth didn't reach her eyes. Luckily they entered the lobby before the conversation could continue. As soon as they were in sight, Randy shepherded everyone out to the waiting bus for their tour of De Haar Castle.

As soon as the bus pulled away, Randy took the microphone. "Happy Mother's Day, ladies. We have a special treat lined up for you today. It should be a day to remember."

Oh, no, thought Lana. In the stress of the past few days, she had forgotten that today was Mother's Day. She hoped Gillian was holding up. Lana feared that if she couldn't come up with another viable suspect soon, her mother's stay in Holland would be extended indefinitely. Lana swore if she managed to set Gillian free, Mother's Day would become their most important holiday, one that they would always celebrate together.

She tuned back into Randy's speech. "Our tour of the castle will be followed by a scrumptious meal in a historic café. Traffic is light, meaning we should be there in about a half hour."

Lana gave Randy a thumbs up as he set down the microphone. As he passed, he squeezed her shoulder and whispered in her ear, "Don't worry, Lana. The police will figure out soon enough that Gillian didn't harm Priscilla."

Lana nodded in response, afraid her voice would crack if she tried to speak. She was so glad that Randy was here to lead the tour. Her mind had been focused on her own mother's predicament far more than her guests' happiness, and she felt terrible for ignoring them. Luckily Dotty was again in good health and spirits, happily chatting with everyone on the bus as if they were old friends. *It is too bad for Dotty that she doesn't feel comfortable leading tours anymore*, Lana thought, *she is a natural at it.*

As they rode to the castle, Lana stared outside the window, but she wasn't interested in the scenery. All she could think of was who else would have wanted both Daphne and Priscilla dead. Lana was a bit shocked to see that no one really cared about Daphne's demise. Even more surprising was Paige's presence on today's tour. To Lana it felt odd that Priscilla—the person who had invited her along and paid for her trip—was dead, yet Paige was acting as if she was just another guest.

When their bus was about halfway to the castle, Tammy stood up and shouted, "Hey everyone, I have some wonderful news. My boss just messaged me. I'm going to get my bonus after all. Isn't that fantastic?"

Her daughter began cheering. "Way to go, Mom!"

Dotty and Sally clapped out of politeness, and a few others joined in.

"Hey, Dotty," Tammy called out, "you can look forward to seeing me and Hadley more often, after this deal goes through."

"Great," Dotty responded.

Lana hid her smile with the back of her hand. Based on Dotty's lukewarm reaction, she was not looking forward to seeing more of the pair.

Tammy's enthusiastic reaction reminded Lana that Priscilla really had been the only thing standing in the way of her receiving her coveted bonus. How Daphne might have fit into Tammy's murderous plans, Lana did not know, but she aimed to find out during today's tour.

Their guide was waiting for them in an enclosed courtyard where horses and carriages used to be kept. Now it functioned as the café, museum shop, and entrance to the castle beyond.

From here, they could see the entire castle and the outlying buildings. Lana was immediately enchanted by the fairy-tale structure. The L-shaped castle was covered with a multitude of turrets and gables. The many windows sported red-and-white wooden shutters, and the edge of the roof was lined with coats of arms. It was surrounded by a vast moat that reflected the impressive structure in its waters. An open drawbridge and bridges offered access to the castle's main entrance.

Lana and her group followed their guide through the formal French gardens covering much of the property. In the distance she could see a thick forest that was apparently popular with hikers and biking enthusiasts.

They walked slowly through the French gardens, taking in the rose bushes, triangular shrubs, and many colorful flower beds lining the gravel path. The designs reminded Lana of a previous trip to Versailles.

"De Haar Castle has a long and extensive history, as most castles do, but it had fallen into ruins by the time it was acquired by the Van Zuylen family. The buildings you see here today are not based on the original structure; they were designed to be a romantic, if not flamboyant, version of what a castle should be. This was at the request of the owners, Baron Etienne van Zuylen van Nijevelt van de Haar and Baroness Hélène de Rothschild. To create their dream castle, they hired the most famous architect in the Netherlands at the time, Pierre Cuypers, who was also responsible for designing the Centraal Station and Rijksmuseum in Amsterdam."

As they approached the castle, their guide pointed out the family's private church, a simple stone building with a tall steeple standing next to the castle's entrance. He led them over the open drawbridge straddling a moat surrounding the castle. They then crossed another drawbridge, this one lined with stone statues, to reach the entrance.

When Lana entered, her brain experienced sensory overload. Every surface was decorated with painted tiles, stone carvings, and wooden accents in a mishmash of styles and colors. It was beautiful and ugly all at the same time.

Lana trailed behind her group, politely listening to their guide describe the castle's extensive history. When they entered a large, central hall that their guide called the Knight's Hall, Lana paused to take in the over-the-top decorations. One wall was built to look like that of a Gothic church, complete with stone arches and stained glass windows featuring knights and ladies. Several stone statues were dotted around the space, and a suit of armor holding a lance and ball of chains stood at attention. A staircase carved out of white stone wound around the walls of the room and up to the second floor.

When the guide began ascending the stairs, Lana's phone began vibrating in her pocket. It was an unknown number; Lana assumed it was the publishing house getting back to her. Luckily Dotty was close by.

"Dotty, I need to take this. I'll catch up with you in a minute, okay?" Lana called out as she pointed to her phone.

Dotty bobbed her head as she answered. "Lana Hansen speaking."

"Hi, Lana. This is Julie from Zeus Publishing. I heard the voicemail you'd left Saturday morning and wanted to touch base with you. A biography about a corporate leader such as Priscilla Andersen is an excellent proposal, but I don't think we are the right company to query. Our focus is on fiction, not nonfiction."

"Excuse me? I think there's been some confusion. I wasn't proposing a book idea. I am calling about one of your employees, Paige Bronski. She is currently writing the biography on Priscilla Andersen."

"I'm sorry, you must be mistaken. We haven't commissioned a biography about Andersen or any other corporate leaders. And even if we did, Paige certainly wouldn't be the one writing it," Julie said with a laugh.

"What do you mean? Does Paige work for your company or not?"

"Yes, as a receptionist. We hired her through a temporary employment agency five months ago. Why are you asking?"

Lana was flabbergasted. Why on earth would Paige lie about her credentials and intentions to Priscilla? Was it just to get a free trip to the Netherlands? Or was there a more sinister reason?

When she recovered from her shock, Lana said, "I am asking because she is here on a tour I am leading in the Netherlands. She claims to be a ghostwriter assigned by Zeus Publishing to pen a biography about Priscilla Andersen, a former CEO of McGruffin Wood, as part of your The Person Behind the Success series."

"She what?"

Lana held the phone back from her ringing ear as the representative's shrill scream reverberated through the international line.

"Paige is certainly not working for us as a ghostwriter. I cannot believe that girl used our company in this lie of hers! That is a dangerous misrepresentation of our name. And is a reason for dismissal, in my book. I will inform our lawyers and see if we can take legal action against her, as well."

Her reaction shocked Lana into silence. Before she could respond, Julie said curtly, "Thank you for letting us know."

It sounded like Julie was ready to end the conversation. "Wait, before you go, I am calling because both Priscilla and her daughter, Daphne, have died during this tour. I don't know that Paige had a hand in either death, but she is acting quite suspicious. If you can help me figure out why she would be lying about working for you as a ghostwriter, it may help the police figure out why Priscilla and Daphne were murdered."

Julie was silent a moment, then softly answered, "I wouldn't know where to start. Paige is an odd duck, but she doesn't seem dangerous to me—more lonely. She obviously craves affection and affirmation. What do you want to know?"

Lana reviewed her mental list of questions. "Has Paige ever mentioned Priscilla Andersen before?"

"Not that I'm aware of. I spoke to her briefly most mornings, but our conversations didn't go much further than the weather and traffic. Although…" Julie's voice trailed off.

"Yes?" Lana hoped Julie had recalled something of importance.

"When Paige came to me a few weeks ago and asked for this time off, she was really excited, which was a change from her usual mopey state. Paige is normally a quiet, almost mousy woman, and it's easy to forget she is in the room. It was so sudden, I thought she'd met a man. But she said that she was finally meeting her biological mother. The other receptionists said she kept rambling on about how she couldn't wait to meet the woman, so much so they wished that Paige would crawl back into her shell and shut up. But as far as I know, Paige never mentioned her mother's name."

"Oh, wow." Lana leaned against the stone wall as the simple truth struck home. Paige and Priscilla's physical similarities weren't coincidence after all. She must have made up that lie about writing a biography in order to get closer to Priscilla and learn more about what she believed was her biological family.

Lana's heart went out to the writer. Paige had set her sights on finding her biological mother because she expected that person could give her the unconditional love she was longing for. And yet her search ended with Priscilla, one of the least caring or sympathetic people Lana had ever met.

"That poor girl," Lana mumbled.

"Excuse me?"

"Nothing, sorry. Thank you, this explains quite a bit. I believe Priscilla was her biological mother, which would explain why she pretended to be a biographer. I don't think Paige meant any harm when she used your publishing house's name. It was just a way to get closer to Priscilla and be able to ask about her family, without raising suspicion."

The line was silent as Julie contemplated Lana's explanation. "Okay, well, unless Paige uses our name again, I won't tell my boss about this."

Before she could hang up, Julie added, "Was Paige happy to meet her mother? Did they get along, as she hoped?"

Lana flirted with telling her the truth but couldn't see a reason to do so. "I think Paige is happy to have met her."

39

Dealing with Rejection

As Lana walked back to her group, she considered her suspect list. Now that she knew why Paige had lied about her job, Lana could scratch her off of it. But what about Anne and Tammy? No matter how she turned it, neither woman had reason to harm Daphne, only Priscilla. With no other viable suspects, Gillian was never going to go free.

She caught sight of her group going into a room on the second floor. Lana darted through the crowds of tourists to catch up. She found them in a formal dining room, where their guide was explaining more about the last owners of the castle.

"Hélène de Rothschild's father, banker Salomon de Rothschild, died unexpectedly when she was nine months old. By all accounts, her mother, Adèle, was quite strict and distant. Their relationship was already strained when Hélène chose to marry a Roman Catholic, Baron van Zuylen. Her mother disowned her for marrying outside the Jewish faith. She even bequeathed Hélène's family home, the Hôtel Salomon de Rothschild, to the French state to prevent Hélène from inheriting it."

Wow, and I thought Gillian and I had a strained relationship, Lana thought. When she looked around at her guests to see what they thought, she noticed that Paige was crying. As the guide continued to recount all of the humiliations Hélène suffered at her mother's hands, Paige's sniffles turned to sobs.

"How can any mother reject their own child?" she muttered, then ran out of the room.

The guide's words must have hit Paige hard. Lana felt bad for the young woman. Paige had finally found the mother she'd been longing for, and it turned out to be Priscilla. Had she even known that Paige was hers? Had the writer gotten up the courage to tell her, before she fell off the windmill? And if she had, how had Priscilla reacted? The woman had constantly berated and belittled her own daughter, Daphne; Lana couldn't imagine she would have treated Paige much differently.

Lana scanned the room until she found Randy. He was staring at the door Paige fled through, his face etched with worry.

"I'm going to go see if Paige is alright."

He looked so relieved. "I appreciate it, Lana."

As she turned towards the doorway, Lana heard Sally say to Dotty, "That poor girl. It's a good thing Hélène de Rothschild found herself a loving husband. Having a mother reject you like that will mess with your psyche."

"But you can't make someone love you, even if they should, can you?" Dotty replied, while gazing knowingly at Sally.

Lana knew firsthand how infatuated Sally had been with her previous boyfriend, Carl, and how his rejection had crushed her soul.

Sally nodded. "I know that now. My previous boyfriends weren't interested in much more than my bank account. But I can imagine it's far worse when a parent rejects a child. That must create some sort of black hole in your soul that is mighty hard to fill."

Lana thought of Gillian as she navigated around the other tour groups pouring into the room. Their relationship was far from perfect, but still fixable. And despite all they had gone through, Gillian had not cut her out of her life completely. She only hoped her mother wouldn't be spending the rest of her days in a Dutch prison.

Lana's mind turned to Paige and Priscilla, wondering why she had given her child up for adoption. She thought back on their interview sessions and Priscilla's request to have Paige leave the tour. That evening, Priscilla had gotten into a horrible fight with someone in her room about one of her past mistakes and her refusal to acknowledge it. Her visitor had been screaming about why Priscilla had given something up. It must have been about the baby, and her visitor must have been Paige!

Her conversation with Julie from Zeus Publishing suddenly put that fight in a whole new light. What if Paige had told Priscilla that she was her mother, only to have Priscilla demand that she leave instead of wrapping her up in a hug? That would have angered Paige, for sure. All of those years searching and all that money spent on a private detective, and when she did find her biological mother, she was rejected again. *It would be too much for anyone to bear*, Lana figured.

Lana thought back to what Paige had said about her adoptive parents while on their trip to Giethoorn and their fear that her biological mother would love Paige so much that she would forget about them. Nothing could have been further from the truth.

Would being rejected by the mother she'd always dreamed about make her angry enough to kill? It could have, Lana conceded.

But why did Daphne have to die as well? Priscilla was quite wealthy; it could have something to do with who would inherit her possessions.

If she was going to set her mother free, she had to get to the truth. And right now, Lana saw only one way to do so. She had to confront Paige with her suspicions about her being adopted and see how she responded.

When Lana saw Paige sitting in the corner of the staircase on the first floor, she had her arms wrapped around her torso and was rocking gently as tears streamed down her cheeks.

Lana approached Paige and asked, "How did Priscilla react when you told her that you were her daughter?"

Paige looked up at Lana through puffy red eyes. "She called me a liar."

"I am so sorry. I can imagine that it hurt to hear her say that." Paige looked so forlorn. Lana sat down next to her and tried to wrap an arm around her shoulder.

Paige jerked her body away and stood up. "Really? You can imagine how that felt? Your mother treats you like a human being, not an inconvenience."

"How did you find Priscilla? Through that private investigator?"

"No, he was a waste of money. My adoptive parents had the adoption papers in their attic the whole time. But Dad refused to share the information with me so I didn't find it until they both died. They were afraid I would rather be with Priscilla and forget about them, but they didn't understand my need to have both."

"Did you show her the paperwork that proved she was your mother?"

"I tried to, but she refused to look at it. When I asked her why she left my father's name blank, she told me that he was married with kids of his own. She didn't want to embarrass him. That's why she gave me up."

Lana tried to imagine the depths of Paige's pain. "Did you push Priscilla off the windmill?"

"Yes," Paige whispered. She almost sounded relieved. Then she looked up at Lana and smiled.

"I told you about what Priscilla did in the hopes that you would push her over in a fit of anger. It almost worked, but your mom intervened. After you rushed off, I thought all hope was lost, until tourists began screaming about bombs and terrorists. Everyone on the observation deck was running towards the exit. Then all of a sudden, Priscilla and I were alone."

Paige stopped speaking and closed her eyes, shaking her head as the memories flooded back.

"There she was, crouched up against the railing, holding her throat from where you'd tried to strangle her. When I offered her a hand, she refused. Another rejection. And then she asked me why I was still on the tour. Can you believe it?" Paige's brittle laughter tore at Lana's soul.

"When she rose, I pushed her over, and she fell against one of the blades. The timing was perfect."

Lana felt sick to her stomach.

"All I wanted was a mother who would love me unconditionally," Paige continued. "Like mothers are supposed to do. Priscilla wasn't capable of that. She was a cruel, despicable woman. I wish I'd never met her."

"But why did Daphne have to die? Because of the inheritance?"

"She never would have accepted me as her sister, as Priscilla's real daughter. She treated me like a nuisance, just like Priscilla did. She would have contested my claim on the inheritance, even though I had more right to Priscilla's fortunes than Daphne did."

Lana considered all Paige had said. It wouldn't be enough for her to go to the police herself; she needed Paige to make a statement to the authorities if she wanted Gillian to go free. Given the circumstances, she hoped the police would be lenient with Paige, or at least offer her mental health counseling. It sounded like she really needed professional help.

Before Lana could figure out how to talk her into going to the authorities, Paige raced up the steps so quickly that she was around the first bend before Lana could react.

Lana stood up and screamed, "Stop her!" as she tried to follow. A large tour group began descending the staircase, making her pursuit difficult and slow going. She wove through the Dutch tourists, offering excuses as she stepped around them. By the time she made it to the second level, Paige was already halfway up the third.

"Paige, you can't get away!" she screamed, hoping it was true. For all Lana knew, there was a way out onto the roof. From there, Paige could easily climb down the many turrets and gables to a lower level and spring into the moat. By the time Lana could warn anyone, Paige could have disappeared into the forest surrounding the castle.

Paige ignored Lana, instead leaping up the last set of stairs just as Lana found an opening in the crowd and surged forward towards her prey. When she was only an arm's length away, Paige hurdled over a young child in her attempt to get away. The child's father was not pleased and began yelling his disapproval in Dutch. When neither woman slowed to apologize, he reached out to get Paige's attention just as she sprung up onto the wide stone railing in an attempt to circumvent the crowds.

The man's arm unwittingly sent her off balance. Paige's arms flailed as she attempted to regain her balance, to no avail. Lana could do nothing but watch as Paige fell backwards towards the Knight's Hall below. Instead of hitting stone, her body fell onto the suit of armor, its lance piercing her torso.

Lana looked away too late, the image already emblazoned onto her eyeballs.

She screamed in anguish, horrified to see a life snuffed out so easily.

40

Extra Guest at Breakfast

May 10—Day Nine of the Wanderlust Tour in Amsterdam

When Lana entered the breakfast room for the group's last meal together, she wasn't sure what to expect. It certainly wasn't seeing Alex sitting across from Dotty and Randy. When they had said goodbye a week ago, he'd promised to come back to Amsterdam before they left but hadn't gotten in touch with Lana since, leaving her feeling unsure and slightly confused as to his intentions. Seeing him again took her breath away.

Alex rose to meet her, smiling shyly. "Hi. I took the early train up this morning so I could join you for breakfast."

Lana felt light in the head. "I'm glad you did. It's great to see you again." She could feel her cheeks burning, aware that everyone seated at the table was staring at them. "Are you flying back to Seattle today?"

His grin faltered. "No, I'm leading a week-long training session in London before I can head back. I was hoping we could see each other again, once I'm home?"

Yes, Lana screamed in her head, wanting to grab him tight. In light of her friends watching attentively, she instead said, "I would love that."

Alex leaned in and kissed her softly on the cheek. Lana felt her insides melting again, when she noticed Franny and Frieda entering.

Oh great, she thought, *I finally meet the man of my dreams and a model is on the tour*. When they came over to say hello and Lana introduced them to Alex, she was worried that Franny's presence would blind him to her own. To Lana's delight, when Alex politely shook Franny's hand, he didn't seem to be fazed by her beauty.

"Lana, I won't be flying back with you today," Frieda stated loudly, ensuring all of the guests in the room could hear her. "My daughter, Francesca, invited me to stay for another week. She's working during Amsterdam's Fashion Week and got me a VIP pass for the whole show! I get a name badge and everything."

Frieda was so happy she was glowing. It was also the first time she'd acknowledged her daughter's career since the tour began, Lana realized. Sharing Franny with the rest of the world was obviously difficult on Frieda. Despite all of her bluff and bluster, deep down Frieda missed her daughter terribly.

Once Franny and Frieda walked off to the buffet, Alex turned back to Lana and placed an arm over her shoulder. Lana breathed a sigh of relief, glad he only had eyes for her.

"He's a keeper," Dotty whispered to Lana so loudly that Alex began to blush.

When Sara stormed into the breakfast room moments later, she looked mad enough to spit nails. Anne trailed slowly behind, her head hung low.

She must have told her mom the truth, Lana figured.

Sara made a beeline for Frieda and announced, "You are right, Frieda. Anne has been sponging off of me for months."

Frieda set down her plate and wrapped an arm around her friend, whose shoulders were already trembling from her sobs. "Now, now, there's no reason for getting so upset," she soothed.

"Her company wasn't on the verge of bankruptcy after all. She just wanted someone to do her washing up and cooking for her. I kicked her out, Frieda," Sara said resolutely, glaring at her daughter as she spoke.

When Anne tried approaching her mother, Sara hissed, "Try doing your own laundry for a change."

Anne did an about-face and sat at the table farthest from her mother, turning to face the window.

Lana was glad Anne had told her mom, if only to save their relationship from suffering the same fate as Lana and Gillian's had. Both would need time away from each other to heal, Lana figured, though she doubted it would take long. They needed each other. Lana went over to her guest.

"Can I get you a coffee, Anne?"

"Yes, thanks, Lana."

Anne looked so miserable. "I know it hurts right now, but you did the right thing. Sara would have discovered the truth, sooner or later. And it's better that she heard it from you."

Anne nodded, keeping her eyes on the table. "I know you're right. But it is going to be a long flight home."

Lana squeezed her shoulder in sympathy, then poured her a coffee. When Lana returned the carafe to the buffet, she saw Gillian entering the breakfast room. Her heart leapt with joy at seeing her mother free again. After witnesses confirmed Lana's account of Paige's confession, the police had looked into Paige's background and discovered her lawyer had filed a claim on Priscilla's possessions, based on the fact that Paige was her biological daughter. Soon after, they had released Gillian from their custody. After Lana had picked Gillian up from the police station, they'd spent the entire evening night catching each other up on the past decade. For the first time in quite a while, Lana felt at peace with her mother. They still had a long way to go, but they were off to a great start.

Mother and daughter walked over to Dotty's table, hand in hand.

"I sure am glad to see you and Lana getting along," Dotty said.

"We had a good conversation last night and promised each other we wouldn't let another decade go by before we meet up again," Gillian said, winking at Lana.

"So why don't you set up a weekly coffee date?" Dotty pushed.

When Lana noticed that Gillian looked trapped, she said, "How about once a month?"

Gillian nodded. "It's a date. I'll have my assistant put you in my agenda."

Lana chuckled, knowing what a big deal that was to her mother. *Small steps*, she told herself. At least they were in contact again.

Lana and Gillian took seats next to Alex.

"Randy told me what happened during the last few days, but I still don't understand why Paige killed Priscilla and Daphne," Alex said.

"From what Paige told me, she was not close to her adoptive parents and had convinced herself that her birth mother would give her the unconditional love she craved," Lana answered.

"After she found out Priscilla was her birth mother, she tried to find a way to get closer to Priscilla, so she could get to know her as a person before telling her that she was her biological daughter. That's why she was pretending to be a biographer. Yet during the trip, I noticed neither Priscilla nor Daphne were actually interested in learning about Paige as a person. They were just using her for the biography. And as most of us know, Priscilla was not the motherly type Paige was hoping to find. Priscilla wasn't interested in, or even capable of, accepting Paige as her own. I think after all Paige had done to find her, being rejected so callously pushed her over the edge. If Priscilla wasn't going to love her as a daughter, then she had to go."

"That is cold."

Lana considered Dotty's words. "I don't know if cold is the right word. All Paige wanted was a family that loved her. Priscilla wasn't capable, and Daphne wasn't interested. I don't condone murder, but I can imagine it must have broken Paige's heart to search so long for her family, only to find these two," Lana said.

"And Daphne? Why did she have to die?"

"Money. Daphne wasn't interested in playing family with Paige and would certainly have contested her claim on Priscilla's inheritance. And Paige wanted her fair share of Priscilla's properties and investments. I did hear Paige on the phone telling someone to file a claim and the police confirmed that her lawyer did submit one on Priscilla's inheritance."

"I knew you were involved with my release, Lana, but I didn't know you'd been investigating the other guests. Thank you for not letting me rot in prison," Gillian said.

Lana finally dared to ask the question on her mind since her mother's release. "Why did you lie about your movements on the windmill to the police? If you had told them the truth, you might have been released without my help."

Gillian sighed heavily and looked away. "Lana, I am ashamed to admit this, but I thought you had snuck back and killed Priscilla. After you ran off, I gave Priscilla a piece of my mind, then chased after you. There were so many people squished around the ladder, but I couldn't find you in the crowd. I stepped back out on the observation deck, thinking you might have gone around to the other side, when I saw someone close to Priscilla. There were still so many tourists rushing around, I couldn't tell who it was, only that they had dark hair."

"Like me and Paige have," Lana said, touching her dark, shoulder-length hair.

"Exactly. The next thing I knew, people were screaming on the lawn, and when I went to the railing and saw Priscilla down below, my first thought was that you had done it. I'm so sorry, Lana; I should have known you wouldn't have, but I was so confused."

Lana couldn't believe it. They had been unwittingly helping and protecting each other, as any mother and daughter should. Lana had never felt closer to Gillian. She pulled her mother in for a hug. For the first time in years, Gillian didn't resist. "I love you, Mom."

"Oh, Lana, I love you, too. More than you know."

Gillian and Lana fell weeping into each other's arms, releasing years of emotional hurt and distrust. When their tears finally subsided, Lana felt better than she had in a decade. When she looked in her mother's eyes and saw love in them instead of wariness, Lana knew their relationship was going to be different from now on.

41

Electric Blue Ruffles

June 2—Seattle, Washington

Lana forced herself to look into the mirror again. The sight before her still made her cringe. She twirled once, taking in the formal dress her mother had sent over, wondering whether this was a test of their newly improved relationship. It was definitely not something she would have picked out herself. In fact, it was quite horrible.

In need of a second opinion, Lana stepped out into the backyard she shared with Dotty Thompson. Her boss and landlord was hanging up sheets and towels to dry in the afternoon sun. The smell of freshly mowed grass and clean laundry swirled in the air.

When Lana opened her front door, Rodney the pug pulled a towel out of Dotty's laundry basket and ran across the lawn with it. He barked in triumph, trailing the cloth after him like a cape. Dotty's Jack Russell terrier, Chipper, raced across the lawn and grabbed the other end, jerking it back and forth. He and Rodney were soon engaged in a tug of war that was sure to be the demise of the kitchen towel. As the two dogs growled and tugged their way around the lawn, they circled Dotty, wrapping the towel around her legs and almost tripping her.

"You rascals, let that go," Dotty scolded. After she'd recovered the towel, she turned to hang it up and noticed Lana, still standing in her doorway.

Dotty's mouth momentarily gaped open at the sight of Lana's dress, before she recovered her composure.

"Oh, don't you look pretty," Dotty said, hiding her grin behind her washing.

Lana smirked. "I dare you to say that like you mean it."

Her boss broke out into a loud guffaw. "You're right. You look like that Chiquita banana dancer. All you need is a fruit basket on your head. And that blue is so electric you appear to be shimmering. Are the rest of the bridesmaids wearing the same thing as you?"

"Apparently my maid of honor dress has an extra layer of ruffles on the sleeves and hips, but otherwise they are the same."

"Well, Gillian sure does have a great sense of humor. Or do you think Barry picked them out?"

"Based on the color alone, I suspect this was Gillian's choice." Lana frowned at the ruffled sleeves, wondering where her mom had found this over-the-top design. It didn't really matter. Since their trip to Amsterdam, Gillian was back in her life, and Lana wasn't going to let a dress ruin their progress. If Gillian wanted her bridesmaids to wear these, she had little choice but to join in.

The day after they returned to Seattle, her mom had invited her over to meet Barry. At first, Lana had been apprehensive about meeting her fiancé, but she soon discovered that Barry was even more nervous about meeting her. Once they both relaxed a little, they got along quite well. It was clear to Lana that Gillian and Barry cared deeply about each other. He was so different from her own father, but still a great match for Gillian qua personality, drive, and temperament. To Lana, it didn't really matter what kind of person Barry was, so long as her mother was happy.

"What time is the wedding?" Dotty asked as she scooped Rodney up and kissed her pug on the nose. He licked her chin in response.

"At four." Lana looked at her watch. "Oops, that means I'm probably going to be late. I wonder where my ride is."

A knock on the gate answered her question. Alex poked his head over their fence and waved at Dotty and Lana.

"Come on in, Alex," Dotty called out, patting her hair curlers into place as she did. Lana couldn't help but grin. Her boss had developed quite a soft spot for Alex. If Dotty were forty years younger, Lana would probably have to fight her for his attention.

Rodney and Chipper danced around Alex's feet as soon as he crossed the threshold. He pulled treats out of his pockets, petting their heads as they greedily gulped back all he had to offer. Next up was Seymour. Alex stroked his fur when Lana's cat brushed up against his leg, leaving a swatch of short black hairs on his neatly pressed pants.

"It's good to see you again, and so soon," Dotty tittered. Alex diplomatically hugged the older lady before crossing over to Lana.

"Hey, gorgeous," he said, having trouble keeping a grin off his face as he examined her outfit. "That's an interesting choice."

"Yes, well, Mom does love bright colors. Do you think she will notice if I tear off the sleeves?" Lana teased.

"Probably. I'd leave them alone for now. You look great, like a real Southern belle. Though I might have to wear my sunglasses if all the bridesmaids are wearing the same color."

"Funny, Mom's never lived in the South," Lana quipped.

Alex pulled Lana in and kissed her gently. She trembled under his touch. "Thanks for inviting me to tag along," he said.

"Thank you for being my plus one." *Alex's smile could melt an iceberg*, she thought.

"Sorry I'm late. Traffic is terrible. Are you ready to go?"

"You bet. Let me get my purse and coat."

Since he had returned from Europe, they had spent almost every day together. Lana was in seventh heaven. He was so warm, funny, and caring that she still couldn't believe he was real.

As she pulled on her jacket, her phone began to ring. Worried it was her mother calling, she pulled it out of her purse. When she saw the caller ID, she grimaced at her phone, mumbling, "That can go to voicemail."

"Aren't you going to answer that?" Alex asked.

"No, it's Frankie again. We have nothing left to say to each other," Lana firmly stated, while wishing Frankie would stop calling her. She had been

Lana's best friend when they both worked as journalists for the *Seattle Chronicle*, but Frankie had also been the first to publicly turn on Lana after their employer had lost the libel lawsuit.

"You're going to have to deal with her sometime," Alex said softly.

"I can't throw sand over what she and the rest of my supposed friends did, no matter how much the newspaper wants me back. Besides, we are going to be late," Lana said brightly, not wanting to deal with any of her former colleagues right now.

The story about Lana's source taking a bribe from McGruffin Wood had broken the day Lana returned from Amsterdam. She was still recovering from the jetlag when reporters began showing up on her doorstep, demanding a comment for their readers and viewers.

Lana had been completely overwhelmed with the attention. To make matters worse, job offers began pouring in the next day, just as Jeremy had predicted, though almost none were for the kinds of investigative reporter positions Lana once cherished, but rather to write opinion pieces and gossip columns. It seemed as if the news establishment was not interested in having her write the sort of in-depth articles she'd loved to work on before getting fired.

The only offer of a real reporting job had come from her former employer. Frankie and two other former colleagues from the *Seattle Chronicle* had been calling Lana on a daily basis, trying to re-establish contact with her, since the article broke.

It was the moment she had dreamed of for the past ten years. Yet now that she was welcome back into the fold, she was not certain whether it was the right path for her. As much as she wanted to let bygones be bygones, she couldn't forget the insulting and disparaging comments her supposed friends gladly made in the press after she had lost the libel case.

Was her reputation still too tarnished for any other major paper to trust her with an investigative job again? Thanks to the lawsuit, any articles with her byline would always come under more scrutiny than those written by her colleagues. And Lana was not certain she could trust another source to do the right thing and not to take a payoff. Until that day came, journalism was not in the cards for her.

I might not be making a fortune leading tours, but I'm happy, Lana thought. Thanks to her job, she got to travel the world, met interesting people, and even had something to write about in her blog.

Life is pretty darn good, Lana realized.

"Are you ready to go?" Alex asked.

"Yep, all set," Lana murmured as Alex kissed her lips.

His touch sent electric waves through her body once again. As Alex took her hand and smiled at her, Lana thought, *Scratch that, life is pretty great.*

THE END

Thank you for reading my novel!
Reviews really do help readers decide whether they want to take a chance on a new author. If you enjoyed this story, please consider posting a review on BookBub, Goodreads, or with your favorite retailer.
I appreciate it! Jennifer S. Alderson

Follow the further adventures of Lana Hansen in ***Death by Bagpipes: A Summer Murder in Edinburgh***—Book Four in the Travel Can Be Murder Mystery Series!

When a trip to Scotland ends in tragedy, travel guide Lana Hansen must sleuth out who murdered her guest before she ends up paying the piper...

Available as paperback, eBook, and Large Print edition.

Acknowledgements

Over the course of the past thirty years, my mother and I have literally traveled the world together. Her first trip abroad was to visit me in Nepal while I was volunteer teaching, and our most recent outing was a weekend in London late last year! I feel pretty lucky to have visited so many wonderful cities and countries with her.

A high tea at the Museum of Bags and Purses was an essential stop whenever my mother visited from America. Unfortunately, only three weeks before this book's publication, the museum announced it would not be able to survive the financial repercussions of the government-required closure (due to the coronavirus) and is not planning on reopening its doors.

I also want to send a big hug to my son and husband for their continued support and love.

Editor Sadye Scott-Hainchek deserves a round of applause for her excellent work on this novel.

Amsterdam has been my home since 2004. The information about the city and tourist sites included in this book is as up-to-date as can be. I truly hope you enjoyed your "visit" to the city!

About the Author

Jennifer S. Alderson was born in San Francisco, grew up in Seattle, and currently lives in Amsterdam. After traveling extensively around Asia, Oceania, and Central America, she lived in Darwin, Australia, before settling in the Netherlands.

Jennifer's love of travel, art, and culture inspires her award-winning Zelda Richardson Mystery series, her Travel Can Be Murder Cozy Mysteries, and her Carmen De Luca Art Sleuth Mysteries. Her background in journalism, multimedia development, and art history enriches her novels.

When not writing, she can be found perusing a museum, biking around Amsterdam, or enjoying a coffee along the canal while planning her next research trip.

Sign up for Jennifer's website [https://jennifersalderson.com/] to receive updates on future releases, as well as two FREE short stories: A Book To Die For (cozy mystery) and Holiday Gone Wrong (mystery thriller).

Books by Jennifer S. Alderson:

Carmen De Luca Art Sleuth Mysteries
Collecting Can Be Murder
A Statue To Die For
Forgeries and Fatalities
A Killer Inheritance

Travel Can Be Murder Cozy Mysteries
Death on the Danube: A New Year's Murder in Budapest

Death by Baguette: A Valentine's Day Murder in Paris
Death by Windmill: A Mother's Day Murder in Amsterdam
Death by Bagpipes: A Summer Murder in Edinburgh
Death by Fountain: A Christmas Murder in Rome
Death by Leprechaun: A Saint Patrick's Day Murder in Dublin
Death by Flamenco: An Easter Murder in Seville
Death by Gondola: A Springtime Murder in Venice
Death by Puffin: A Bachelorette Party Murder in Reykjavik

Zelda Richardson Art Mysteries
The Lover's Portrait: An Art Mystery
Rituals of the Dead: An Artifact Mystery
Marked for Revenge: An Art Heist Thriller
The Vermeer Deception: An Art Mystery

Standalone Travel Thriller
Down and Out in Kathmandu: A Backpacker Mystery

Death by Bagpipes: A Summer Murder in Edinburgh

When a trip to Scotland ends in tragedy, travel guide Lana Hansen must sleuth out who murdered her guest before she ends up paying the piper.

Lana hasn't seen her ex-husband Ron since their divorce was finalized six months earlier. So when they bump into each on the Royal Mile in Edinburgh, she is not exactly jumping for joy.

To make matters worse, Ron threatens a member of her tour group – a beloved and respected magician named Presto the Amazing. Ron is convinced Presto stole one of his magic tricks – the same act that propelled the famous magician into stardom – and swears he will get his revenge. After Presto is scared to death by a group of well-meaning bagpipers, the police suspect he was first poisoned – and that Ron is the culprit!

As much as Lana would love to let her ex-husband rot in prison, she soon discovers that he was not the only one who would prefer to have Presto vanish. Did Ron poison the magician? Or did one of several family members accompanying Presto on the trip, use this vacation to knock off the domineering patriarch?

When another guest is murdered, Lana must decide how far she is willing to go to save the man who broke her heart.

Death by Bagpipes
Chapter One: Welcome Home

August 8—Seattle, Washington

"Lana Hansen, would you move in with me?" Alex Wright was down on one knee, holding a small box in his outstretched hand.

Lana gasped as she stared at the key nestled inside.

"Wow, I didn't see that coming." She dropped onto her couch, and her cat, Seymour, sprung into her lap, sensing she'd want the comfort of his soft fur while processing this shocker. She and Alex had been dating for three glorious months, but she hadn't even considered moving their relationship to the next level.

Alex stood up and snapped the box shut before running a hand through his wavy hair. "I thought you would be pleased."

Lana took his hand and pulled him down onto the couch next to her. "Gosh, I am, trust me. It's just that things are going so great between us right now. Why do we need to rush into living together?"

"Being with you feels so right, I don't see the point of waiting."

Lana brushed her nose against his. "You are the best thing that's ever happened to me, Mr. Wright. Could you give me a few days to digest your offer? It's been pretty hectic lately with back-to-back tours, and I'm not even certain which time zone I'm in. I was hoping we could enjoy a stress-free week together, before you have to fly out to London." Lana had just returned from five weeks of leading tours through Germany, Denmark, and Norway and was drained.

"Sure, okay." Alex smiled as he rested his forehead against hers. "I guess that's why I decided to ask you now instead of waiting until we're both back home from our next assignments. I wish you could join me in London. But the training sessions and networking functions run from early in the morning to late at night. I'm afraid I wouldn't have much time to be with you, even if you did."

"It's the same for me," Lana admitted. "I wish you could come to Spain with me, but we're visiting several cities on this tour and are going to be on the road more than usual. It doesn't seem fair to ask you to come and then not be able to spend time with you."

"I guess it's the nature of our jobs," Alex conceded as he snuggled against her neck.

As much as she would miss him, Lana couldn't wait to visit Spain. Ever since her fellow Wanderlust Tours guides had told her about the Andalucía trip and shown her their pictures, she had been bugging their boss, Dotty Thompson, to let her lead one of those tours.

Lana breathed in Alex's scent, as he moved his mouth up to hers and kissed her tenderly.

"Why don't you fly over to Seville after your job is finished? We can spend a few hours together before my tour starts. It's not much, but it would be wonderful to share some authentic Spanish tapas with you," Lana suggested after she recovered her breath.

Alex brightened up. "I would love that."

"Let me talk to Dotty first. I'm certain she won't have a problem with you being there, but I should let her know what we are thinking before you change your ticket."

"That sounds great. But first, I sure have missed you. We have some catching up to do." Alex pulled her in for another passionate embrace.

"Dotty can wait," Lana murmured as she relaxed into his arms.

A booming voice called out from outside her front door. "Lana, honey? Are you home?" It was Dotty Thompson.

Or perhaps not, Lana thought.

* * *

Are you enjoying the book so far? Why not buy *Death by Bagpipes* now and keep reading. Available as paperback, eBook, and in Kindle Unlimited.

Printed in Great Britain
by Amazon

41862500R00119